The Gilded Chateau

World War II's 5th Suit: Financing the Nazis

Rogue Bankers Playing Bridge in Chateau Rougemont

a novel by
Jon Foyt

Andrew Benzie Books
Walnut Creek, California

Published by Andrew Benzie Books
www.andrewbenziebooks.com

Printed in the United States of America

First Edition: September 2017

10 9 8 7 6 5 4 3 2 1

ISBN 978-1-941713-54-9

Cover and book design by Andrew Benzie

This novel is dedicated to Helen,
who has imbued me with a sense of compassion
and a renewed love of life as I search for its deepest meanings.

TABLE OF CONTENTS

AUTHOR'S OBSERVATION

With many of us older adults concerned about the future for our children and grandchildren in this uncertain world, in this novel a young woman historian delves into one of the world's major questions—why wars? Sara Vogel, researching her PhD dissertation, yearns to find answers for herself and her developing career, as well as for society and the future of civilization. This novel is written with the hope that young people today will continue to cherish the knowledge that history offers and, while pursuing their careers, will value family.

ACKNOWLEDGMENTS

To Deborah Hunt, Library Director of the Mechanics Institute in San Francisco, for her World War II research; to the archivists of the Harvard Business School Library for uncrating the personal papers of Thomas McKittrick, head of the Bank for International Settlements during World War II; to the Hoover Library for the papers of William Hallam Tuck, owner of Chateau Rougemont during the war; to Marlies Kibler of the Mockmuhl Historical Society for uncovering my family heritage; and especially to Richard Voorhees, my thoughtful, challenging, and innovative San Francisco editor, who understood and felt the historical message I wanted to communicate. To each, my most sincere thanks.

The dear old flag, whose faintest flutter flies
A stirring echo through each patriot breast,
Can never coax to life the folded eyes
That saw its wrongs redressed…

—James Whitcomb Riley, 1878

ANOTHER TIME

Overhead, from off in the distance to the west of the chateau, Sara heard an airplane, the unusual but not totally unfamiliar whirring buzz of a propeller-driven craft. She recalled the sound of the occasional private plane landing or taking off from the little runway strip near her James Whitcomb Riley College campus. Uh-oh. The plane's motor was sputtering as if uncertain of its course or its fate. A terrible chill came over her.

CHAPTER ONE:
PRESENT TIME
JAMES WHITCOMB RILEY COLLEGE

Time was running out on James Whitcomb Riley College. Built in the 19th century, the college was named for the beloved Indiana poet. Its campus' historic buildings huddled together as siblings from the same architectural litter. Their common Midwestern Gothic mien, undernourished by lack of foundation grants or alumni contributions, cried out for sustenance. Clinging to the Southern Indiana hill country, believing in safety in numbers, the lot recoiled from the world boiling in the distance, the far—while ever so near—distance. Faith in worldly things adhered to intellectual standards, poetry, the liberal arts, college education, or the truth in life's designs as they knew them. They also seemed to take a certain comfort in faith and fear, solace in the unknown, and buoyancy in a hope nourished by a common belief that overrode their apprehension of the morrow: God was golden. Unfortunately, they needed actual gold to survive. If they didn't get it soon, the institution would rest in peace, where in heaven the streets were paved with the glittering mineral.

*   *   *

Sara, her boyfriend, Manny, and her roommate, Kyra, had gotten to class early. The worn-out college president, Professor Skip Kinkaid, resigned to his institution's inevitable demise from lack of funds, hadn't yet begun what he had announced would be his final class meeting with graduating students. Set for their cap-and-gown commencement event days away, the three students expected that, in his by-now fatigued way, he would once more try to elicit the enthusiasm of one of them for his historic research project. They were convinced he was priming himself to make what surely would be, as Manny described it to Sara, "His final attempt to lasso one of us, like a helpless calf at the county rodeo grounds. He wants to rope one of our futures—maybe not in eight seconds, but with the bell ringing soon after." Manny added, "It will be success for the roper—that's Kinkaid, but not for the ropee—one of us."

Sara vowed, "I won't allow anyone to lasso me against my will."

Manny followed with, "Then, y'all gotta come out west to Socorro in New Mexico where I'm goin' study for my masters in mining. Their PhD program is exploring breakthrough technology to locate underground minerals—"

"—Yes, you've told me about the penetrating ground radar that will look for gold." Admonishing him, Sara said, "But Manny, you'd leave your elderly grandmother behind here in Indiana—the sweet woman who bankrolled your education and, so she told me, will continue to do so—while you go off searching for gold? How will she, as a woman, as your mother's mother, feel about that? You don't care about her well-being, do you? No, you don't," Sara answered her question.

Manny quipped, "The old gal? What's she goin' do with her money anyway?"

Sara shot back, "She's a human being just like you. Where's your respect?"

He said, "She's just a woman."

To which Sara cringed and said, "So am I. Didn't your grandmother teach you the Golden Rule?" He looked closely at her and nodded, displaying the typical smug possessive male smile from which Sara was growing to feel alienated.

"Sure," he said. "She taught me that whoever gets the gold makes the rules."

"As for me," Sara told him, "after I get my PhD at the big state university, I plan to focus on writing my own version of history." In his mind that would be that, she thought, reminding herself that she never intended to go with him to New Mexico. By now in their college relationship, she knew he knew that but, like a typical hormone-driven male, he wouldn't give up on trying to date her or other campus cuties spotted in his sexist sights. In seriousness, she told him, "You may be into gold, but I'm renewing my dedication to 20th Century history." She added, "As seen through my female gender gaze. That's going to be the focus of my dissertation, now that Professor Kincaid has helped me get into the PhD program at IU. It's all going to be cool."

Manny laughed derisively, causing Sara to add, "In my studies under Professor Kincaid, I've come to view history, not from the traditional male point of view, but from my own female perspective." Yes, she reminded herself, it was her unique approach to the story of history, which she wanted to remake into her story. She reflected on how, during her days of lectures, research, and discussions with faculty, she had often told president Kinkaid, "My impression of history is that men make it, then other men choose what people—also men—write about. Following my graduate degree, I'll pursue my feminist observations about history and the people who made it. I want to move beyond male machismo. I'm going to write true history while wearing a pink bow..." she gestured... "in my blonde hair."

Manny continued his negative bent, "You women are all alike—saying it's your female world."

"Remember, in that senior-year seminar, the assignment was to parse the American Revolution?"

"Yeah."

"My assignment from Professor Morris was to find what roles women played in those 1776 years in overthrowing the male British yoke."

"Probably none other than—"

"—Well, on a foot-long space in the library stacks, I came across three volumes compiled by the Daughters of the American Revolution. They listed the names of thousands of women who played roles in the Revolution. I got an A Plus in that seminar. I concluded my class paper by writing, 'The farther we go back in history, the less we come to know about women.' The 1700's female revolutionaries blazed the way for the suffragettes in England and later our own Women's Movement."

Manny said, "Your mother never told you about the Women's Movement—all that stuff?"

Sara replied, "My mother raised my older brother and me as a single parent. As I've told you, my father didn't live with us to help out. But he did send money from Switzerland." She added thoughtfully, "Professor Morris said, 'Good reference material may be hidden away. It's a treasure hunt. You must search.' That's what I want to do—a career of research, treasure hunting, and writing."

Manny said, "I want to hunt for treasure, too. The real kind."

As she mulled over her nascent literary goals in reaction to his comment, Sara thought a bit nervously about graduate school. She had no definite plan for after that and no prospects of a job. Not yet.

*   *   *

At the top of the hour, Professor Kincaid slowly seated himself at his desk and called the class to attention. His demeanor, his darting eyes, his evident to them desperation made it seem that he was about to plead with them. Once again he would try to get one of them to commit to pursue his long-abandoned project.

Reacting to Professor Kinkaid making eye contact with each student one by one, Sara whispered to Manny. "Not again! The old guy won't give up. He's still looking for some student to take over his research project."

Manny said, "Like I won't give up on you."

Her planned dismissive reply was preempted by the professor calling out in a throaty summons, "Ms. Vogel!"

"Sir?" Sara hesitated, looking away from her cowboy boy and toward the authoritative voice of age. Honoring college protocol, she said, "Thank you, Professor Kinkaid, but by now everyone surely must have told you—"

"—You've changed your name."

Startled, Sara asked herself why is he saying that in front of the students? Did Kinkaid anticipate a denial, or did he expect her to acknowledge the name change? And why now?

Before she could reply, he said in a soothing tone, "Not you, Sara, your grandfather—I found this." He held up a paper so everyone could see the swastika in the upper right hand corner. Soothingly, appearing to be mindful of her feelings, he went on, "Today there's no reason to hide the fact. We are not—I mean, you and your family are not back in Nazi Germany in those dark days of the 1930s."

Sara whispered to Kyra, "What is he suggesting?"

CHAPTER TWO:
KINKAID'S PROJECT

Professor Skip Kinkaid's favorite activity in his academic career had been teaching his beloved history classes, especially to his favorite students, ones he thought offered promise and might develop into historians. On top of that, as college president he had simultaneously tried his best to be an administrator, or so it had seemed to staff and students. His intensity at both efforts had demonstrated his devotion to this small liberal arts college.

But now, given the school's deteriorating money situation, Sara realized the sun was setting on this school of higher learning and on this man and his teaching career. She had wondered aloud to her roommate, Kyra, "Where can an unemployed elderly college president from a soon-to-be defunct college get a job teaching or doing anything productive and intellectual?" With compassion, Kyra had acknowledged Kinkaid's late-in-life challenge.

To Kyra, Sara recalled saying, "As to this favorite project of his, perhaps he hasn't had time to pursue it."

"Or perhaps he has grown too old…"

"What is too old?" Sara had asked. Mindful of Kinkaid's revelation of her name change, coming out of the closet, she said, "Kinkaid is going to press the matter of his project." Getting a return nod of agreement from Kyra, Sara added, "With one of us… that is, especially me." She asked her roommate, "Is it possible he wants to mentor me by directing my PhD dissertation along the lines of his project?"

From Kyra, she received a "yes" followed by, "Roomie, I know you well. You are a thoughtful student attracted to unusual topics hidden in the crevasses of history."

Reacting, Sara thought that, given completion of her postgraduate program in what she hoped would be her near future, she would be credentialed as a PhD historian bent on expressing history from the woman's point of view. Still, she had to define what exactly that was. And when and how would she be able to pursue her objective? It certainly meant highlighting specific women's contributions to society and to world events.

Kyra asked, "Didn't Kinkaid tell you that you write well?"

"He did. Just the other day he complimented my research skills."

"In both primary and secondary sources." Kyra smiled, "We've each learned the difference."

To herself, Sara acknowledged that Kinkaid had taught her well. She had recently told him so. Not smiling, he had nodded and then confessed, "I want to tell you, Sara, that I am growing tired, like this college. It and I are past our time. I've taught history, political, and economic. I've tried to keep the faculty on track. I've worked hard to encourage and motivate each of you students. And—most important as president—and without the usual PhD degree—I've worked hard to support the college. All this with too little time and too little staff. The result is I've come up short on raising money from wealthy alumni and institutions."

Wrapped up in the angst of her own nascent career, which she was hoping was about to get a boost down the line from her PhD degree, how could she express her empathy for the fact that Kinkaid's career was apparently over and done with? Or how could she show sympathy for age? Sara was at a loss to answer because age, older age, was to her an unfamiliar concept. Yet, in his role of mentor to her and to other students, Kinkaid could look back on the age time chart. He had once been here, calendar-wise young, walking along what was Sara's current path and at her age.

*   *   *

Now, looking at his students from behind his ever-so-crazy desk, Kinkaid rose from his timeworn tattered chair. Elevating his 6 foot-plus frame, he grimaced with the pain of what he often referred to as "my sciatica." Slowly adjusting to the discomfort that went with standing after sitting for a spell, he again surveyed the youthful faces gathered before him.

Fleetingly Sara recalled episodes in several of the classes she and Kyra had been in. He had been so intent on conveying his take on history—the nuances, the mindset of the men, and a few women,

6

making up the history story—that Sara marveled at how this older male teacher could become so enthralled with teaching, with instructing the young minds before him. She had envied the man and his skills.

Diverting her thoughts, Manny gestured at the absurd abomination that served as Kinkaid's desk. He whispered to Sara and Kyra, "Anyone who has removed the tracks from a mobile World War II Bofors antiaircraft gun made in Sweden and transformed it into his office desk has to be nutty as a Hoosier fruitcake at Christmas time!" Looking at Sara and then at her roommate Kyra, he added in his Southern New Mexico drawl, "Don't y'all agree?"

Sara's retort was muffled by Kinkaid's nervous clicking of the controls on what they all feared was his still-working anti-aircraft weapon. She almost expected the ominous gray gun to fire a shell through the ceiling. Except there was no enemy aircraft overhead, nor was there likely to be any aircraft, friend or foe, in this remote part of the USA. Gesturing at the gun barrel hovering over the crazy desk, Sara said softly to her young man, "Kinkaid told me that all his life he's felt like he's been 'working under the gun'."

Kyra pointed toward the desktop. "But he's never told us what's with the gold bullion displayed inside that bolted down Plexiglas case. What's up with it?" Brushing back strands of her long auburn hair, Kyra said, "Strange, no one has talked about heisting the ingot."

"Maybe he's going to apply the gold bar to reduce the college debts," Manny said. "Not that it will make much difference, the debts being much bigger than one gold ingot."

Sara said, "Neither the gold bar nor his academic reputation has lured one of us to want to pursue his pet project."

Manny said, "Anybody ever look at that ingot up close?"

"No one," Kyra said, "that I know of. You?"

"Yeah," he said. "Through the Plexiglas. Can't get any closer. But I can see it's got some sort of imprint on it."

"Ingots have to come from some place. They don't grow on trees."

"Not in Southern Indiana."

"What's it tell us?" Sara asked.

"Where it's from," Manny said. "Maybe he heisted it from the Bank of Indiana, if there is such a bank."

"There isn't," Kyra said.

"Wanna bust open the Plexiglas?" Manny laughed.

Kyra said she didn't want to do that and then asked her roommate, "What would you think, Sara, if Kinkaid threw that ingot into his deal with you to work on his research project? Maybe then you'd consider being part of it."

Sara's eyebrows rose.

CHAPTER THREE:
SARA'S FAMILY NAME

Moments later, with curiosity, Kyra looked at Sara. "Why on earth did your grandfather change your family name? I guess it was the Nazis."

Sara, whose blonde curls accentuated her Teutonic azure eyes, nodded slightly, signifying agreement. She turned away from Kyra and looked up to see Kinkaid striding slowly toward her with obvious pain-tinged strides. Closer, he said to her, "von Reichard. That is your family name, not Vogel. The prefix 'von' often signifies royalty, or having descended from royalty."

Sara replied, "But Professor Kinkaid, why is my former family name of any importance? My name's Vogel now."

Kinkaid pointed to his printout sheet and said, "I'll tell you why. It was the Nazis with their required genealogy family tree document, like this one." He pointed to the form with its swastika in the corner. "In the 1930s, every family was required to fill out one of these and, upon demand, present it to the Gestapo to show they weren't Jews."

"So I was told by my brother Jack," Sara said, her reply almost automatic as tears began to glisten on her cheeks.

In a show of sympathy, Kinkaid hesitated before going on, "Yes, we're so sorry for your loss." He waited and then said, "Please tell us more about your family, Ms. Vogel. The past is not to fear." He raised his voice and addressed the students with the oft-used JWR college mascot name, "Poets, silence your tablets and phones and listen to what Sara has to tell us."

Mini screens went dark. Male and female looked at Sara, curious to know.

Sara asked herself if she was on trial for some social infraction? That's the last thing a graduate wants to confront on the brink of deciding upon a theme for her dissertation. She began to worry about her post-doctorate life. It would consist of student loan payments along with the uncertainty of her career. There was to be the final year or maybe more time in Bloomington. Once enrolled there, with Kincaid's pledged help and faculty endorsements, she could select an historical research topic with emphasis on the female viewpoint. That was a dream scenario from that reflective day when she sat on the bluff and watched the mighty Ohio River flow forcefully and majestically westward.

Yet now there came to her the thought, albeit murky, of the possibility that Kinkaid's stymied research project might offer her the topic and opportunity to outline her dissertation proposal. She thought, "Maybe it could even launch my post-doc career."

Sara comforted herself as she turned to the students in the classroom and said, "Lots of people change their names... movie starts... celebrities."

Recalling what she had learned from her brother Jack about her family's past, Sara's inner thoughts rang with the judgment of retribution, "Damn the Nazis! Damn that war! Damn all fighting!" Out loud she professed, "Back then, had women been in charge, none of those evil war episodes would have happened." To herself, she concluded that if women were in charge today, Jack would still be alive.

Kinkaid smiled and said, "Women? Yes? But who—which woman or what women? The 1930s were days of male supremacy. As to your grandfather, I looked him up. He was a member of German royalty." Kinkaid repeated, "Von Reichard. Today we would respectfully address him as Prince von Reichard."

Sara recalled from her brother's information that in the heyday of German royalty, important people—those being royal—made up the ruler's courts in each of the small German states prior to those little principalities coming together in German unification. She said, "But today German royalty are lost in the time-worn pages of history. It's only those cute photogenic royals in the UK who are of any interest."

Kinkaid nodded. "That may be." With promise apparent in his voice, he said, "But I can tell you that German royalty are dynamic players in my project."

Sara thought about women being royal and laughed. "Dynamic? Come on, Professor, we all know—"

"—You don't know." She was surprised at the strength, perhaps a touch of anger in his voice. "How many times have I insisted that the real study of history lies in going beyond fable and fantasy and determining the reasons why events happened, what was in the minds of the men and women who were the movers and shakers. It is not— as most historians profess—a series of stories embellished to fit the philosophy of a particular writer or lecturer. There's often more depth—a lot more to the story than what appears on the surface. You've got to go beneath the then-and-then of events unfurling in calendar sequence in order to ferret out the reasons for the history story."

"I realize that," Sara said.

Kinkaid went on, "Hear me out! My project, my ever-so-important research project is intended to define the reasons behind the wars of history." Sara noted his voice had shifted from professorial objectivity to an opinionated statement of what he obviously thought to be his mission.

Kinkaid looked, no glared, Sara observed, at each student. He was, she thought, bent on triggering sparks of interest in their minds. In a pleading voice, he cajoled, "You young men and women are the last chance in my life as a history professor and as president of this college to tell the world, to properly paint the picture of war. In my fading years, my paints are drying up, as I am, and as is this college. We're each going to blow away into the dark canyons of history. My theory of history, of why we have suffered from so many wars, will be obscured in the clouds of the muse Clio's indifference, never to be indexed in her extensive bibliography of world events."

"Clio's the goddess of history, one of the nine daughters of Zeus," Kyra whispered to Manny, only to receive in return the expression of a mineralogist, categorizing the subject as scientifically unworthy of his interest.

Then Kyra blurted, "But Mr. Kincaid, why haven't you pursued this special project of yours over the years? If it is so dear, why haven't—"

"—I have… from time to time." With force, he added, "On two occasions. The first time, I perused the libraries—that was before the Internet. It was slow, tedious…"

Sara said, "What did you find?"

Kincaid shook his head. "Not enough. Then I ran out of time. But on the second go-round—that was after I could Google the Internet—I learned about a diary, a memoir written by a woman who lived in Switzerland during World War II. It held out the promise of shedding light on what went on during the war. I hoped her diary would tell about the movement of gold between the nations. That would tell me about the role gold played in financing that war. But then the financial crisis hit our college, and I had no more time. Also, my health took a bad turn." He paused. The room grew silent. Suddenly, to everyone's surprise accompanied by exclamatory gasps, Kinkaid approached closer to Sara. He grimaced from his evident leg and back pain. Alarmingly, he stood right smack in front of her.

She recognized the pleading in his eyes. She saw in his movements the contortions of pain, physical, but also mental in his facial expressions. Compassion overcame her, compassion for his age, compassion for his career, compassion for his person as if he was her child and she his mother entrusted to nurture him. Duty. Her duty. She scolded herself for growing interested in the man and his goals, which by now she realized had to do with gold and its role in World War II. To her, he was yearning to express to the world the scope of his latent project, presumably by enticing one of his students, possibly, yes, probably her, to pursue it. She told herself she had to resist this female instinct for nurturing and then acquiescing to him. After all, Kinkaid was an adult American male. Given his age and masculinity, he could take care of himself without her assistance.

Looking intent, Kinkaid said to her and to the students, "You've all been to the Indiana Symphony Orchestra?" One student raised her hand. Kinkaid went on, "When they play, and the chorus sings Handel's Messiah and they get to the Hallelujah Chorus, the audience, the singers, the musicians—everyone—stands. Tell me, why is that?"

No one answered.

Breaking the silence, he said, "The first time it was played, the King stood up, perhaps simply to stretch". Some laughter. Kinkaid went on, "Of course, in reaction to the king, every one of his subjects was obliged to stand. Today there are no more kings, so, I think there's a deeper significance." He paused. "I suggest it is in tribute to the composer, the orchestra, and the singers, but—more than that— it is recognition that in life, in our existence here on earth, there is something great, so very great beyond. And it is that unknown—that mystical greatness we sense, indeed recognize in our Western Civilization. That's why we stand in order to pay tribute to that something great. It is such abstractions that elevate us above the primates." Still positioned in front of Sara, he said, "You students do want to be above the monkeys, don't you?" Some laughed hesitatingly. "Then find your mission in life and honor it." Sara thought he looked forlorn as he added, "I'm too old now to pursue my project—which is my real mission in life. Maybe one of you will take up the banner and give my life some significance in the annals of history."

Sara caught herself trying once again to rein in her compassion for Kinkaid. She acknowledged she was experiencing emotions for an older man at the same time she was chastising herself for not caring that much about her own distant and enigmatic father. In hindsight, she reminded herself, her father had never seemed to care much about her, not like Kinkaid was doing in front of her and the entire class, seemingly caring deeply about her. And yes, while caring about his special endeavor. In contrast, her father was never home, never there for her. It was as if she was an orphan, except that her mother had been in her life in person, if not in spirit. In a mental spark, Sara asked herself if, in her daughter's mind, Professor Kinkaid was filling the void left by her real father who was off living and working in Switzerland.

In one of Kinkaid's history classes, the assignment had been to read Chris Hedges' book, *War Is a Force That Gives Us Meaning*. That day, referencing the book, she had asked, "But, Sir, how do you reconcile your idea of how history has unfolded after reading this book? Hedges' denounces the propagated myths that continue to entice soldiers to fight and die."

Kinkaid had smiled. "Good for you, Sara. You get it! That's the motivation behind my project—there's much more to war than meets the eye."

CHAPTER FOUR:
PARENTS: THE FATHER

Her professor's comment about war and there being more than what meets the eye caused Sara to turn her thoughts to her father and their last moments together. How rare, yet memorable were their conversations. It was some four years ago before she was to enter college. He was home, albeit briefly to "collect personal papers." Just as suddenly he was off again.

In parting, she remembered him saying, "If you are going to study history, Sara, you must look into the minds of the men living in the time period you are studying. In your own mind, travel back in time to that period where you can feel—sense—the circumstances they faced and the problems they dealt with. The past is the genesis for today's truth—where one's mind must dwell in order to explore events." He had gone on to explain his viewpoint, "Clearly, it is that way in banking. Banking monetizes wealth as it finances property—real estate, personal, and corporate—identifying values that constitute the framework of society, no matter what the political system. Banking is the most important part of our past and our present. The heartbeat of every country lies in its banking system—especially in its central bank. That's why my bank—the Bank for International Settlements—was established in 1930... during those glorious, hopeful years before..."

"Before what, Father?" she had interrupted. She saw him cringe with her question. Why? It was a simple question. She felt she had known the answer but wanted to hear it from him, to learn more about him from what he would say, how he would say it, or maybe not say.

Hesitatingly, he answered in a way that showed her he thought she should have known, "The Nazis and their World War II."

She had wanted him to tell her more and waited.

"The BIS is where I work. In today's world, times are not so simple, not as glorious as they were back then. You see, Sara, I've come to realize that the 1930s were satisfying years. In those days, values—personal and societal—were clear-cut. Virtually nothing was opaque. There were proper and precise sides to be on." Her father had drifted away, perhaps becoming lost in abstract thoughts. Was he deep into a sort of time travel? Yes, studying him, as she had done that day, she thought he visualized himself as momentarily living in that distant time period. He said, "The 1930s were well-defined years." His voice gave way to what seemed a reflective nostalgia.

Sara nodded. "Before the War."

Her father returned the nod. "Guidelines were clear. Religions— our western religions and their dogmas—were front and center. Before all those eastern religions invaded after the war and confused us. In the 1930s, religion and patriotism guided men's thinking. Banking was patriotism. With banking came faith in our social system. Everywhere we were dedicated to our causes, whether socialism, communism, fascism, democracy... to Christianity, Judaism... loyalty to our rulers, whether they were dictators, emperors, kings, queens, mafia dons, or presidents..."

She had wanted to query him further, but then, continuing to express himself, he had turned away to enter the arriving and now waiting taxi, issuing instructions to the driver to take him to the Weir Cook Airport. To her, but mostly to the taxi driver, he went on, "Ah, yes, times were simpler then. Each of us, all of us, understood world events and the course ahead for our lives. Everyone was on the same newspaper page..." She saw the turbaned taxi driver nod obsequiously as, she presumed, he was listening to her father's nostalgic rant. Then once again, her father was away, out of her sight and pretty much out of her mind.

Concurrently, from behind their living room picture window, her mother, trance-like, waved perfunctorily. Sara realized she was really looking out the window because she was waiting for a car, which promptly arrived. Sara watched as her mother's latest clairvoyant, weirdly attired, her dress exotic, emerged, with both her mind and her bag full of magical and alluring tricks.

As she had watched her father's taxi merge into the Indianapolis traffic and disappear down Central Avenue, Sara imagined the first meeting of her father and mother. As a child, she had once asked, "Mother, how did you and Father meet?"

Story was, as her mother, with some embarrassment, Sara had thought, recounted the event: her father was a young teller when her mother had come in to the bank. She was unable to balance her checkbook and lamented that she must be overdrawn. Gallant, her father had helped her with her money matter while being attracted to her. They had dated after that episode, for her father, of course, had known her mother's phone number and address.

Sara had said to her mother, "But you two were not compatible, really, were you? Then? Are you now?" No answer. Only a disbelieving stare. Had older brother Jack ever asked that question? She had posed, "But why did you marry?" Her mother's look was as blank as an overdrawn checking account. Then, "Why did you have me? As well, Jack?" Briefly she wondered if, by going back in time, given her mother's silence, she had hit the question of their marriage status right-on.

Her mother slowly shook her head as if confirming she had no answer or, if she did, wasn't prepared to share it. After that earlier scene, along with her father's disappearing taxi in the traffic of life, both parents pretty much edged out of her mind. Except, of course, for the obligatory JWR college paperwork needed to support her application, as well as the ensuing student loan applications supporting her college program with her soon declared major in history.

CHAPTER FIVE:
PARENTS: THE MOTHER
IN THE SKY

Thinking back about her earlier years, Sara recalled her curiosity bubbling over. It was that day of the big snowstorm, and all the schools were closed. Including her high school. She was stuck in the house, and her mother was waiting for her then clairvoyant to trudge through the snow the few blocks from College Avenue. Not far, but her mother had insisted to Phyllis B. on the phone that she come right away because, "The time is right."

"Mother, why are you trying to connect with your father? He's dead. I mean, years ago." She reached out to hug her mother, and the gesture was returned, albeit briefly, almost as if her show of daughter affection was a suddenly recalled mother-daughter duty.

Her mother said, "You see, Sara, it was that day of the big storm those years ago when the ambulance couldn't get through the snow drifts across our gravel road to get to our farmhouse in time."

"The old home place you've talked about out in Hancock County?"

Her mother smiled an acknowledgment. "One of the perils of remote farm life in those days. It was wintry like today. That's what gives me the same feeling that right now is the time to talk to Mr. Knox."

"Your father?"

"We addressed him that way. Even my own mother did so."

"But why do you—?"

The doorbell chimed. "That's her," and her mother rushed to open the front door. "Come in, Phyllis dear. Shake off the snow. Don't worry about the carpet."

Phyllis B. did so without saying a word. She looked at Sara. Her heavy coat off, Sara saw that PB was dressed in a flowing toga-like shawl with strange designs she had never seen before. Instead of a dress, beneath the toga she wore red and blue striped leggings with the pure white snowflakes clinging to her knees. Her hair was an unusual shade of scarlet and tied in a bun, into which she had stuck an ominous looking gold pin bearing a strange device. She carried a leather valise, which she set on the dining room table. Sara realized that with the ease of her movements, PB had probably executed this routine may times before when Sara was in school. Mother promptly pulled the drapes and almost as quickly lit a host of scented candles in the candelabrum. Scents of herbs and spices soon wafted through the room. "No time to waste," Mother declared as the three sat at the table, silence prevailing.

The magical pungency from the candles soothed Sara. She wanted to ask questions, but refrained in the mood of the moment. PB turned toward her and said, "Young lady, you must believe. Let me quickly explain before we draw nearer to the people of the past."

Sara waited. PB took her hand and held it in her firm grasp. Accompanying what Sara felt was a penetrating stare, which was almost, well, maybe almost hypnotic, PB, her voice suddenly deeper, yet mysteriously distant, said, "You see, Sara, the dead are still there, that is, if we can just feel them, sense them, listen to them, for they want to talk to us here today."

Under the spell, maybe it was a trance, Sara thought she should nod and did, as PB went on, "Tell me, what do you think happens to our soul when we die, to our intangible mind, to our thoughts, to our brain waves, to the knowledge and skills we have accumulated in our lives. Where has all that wisdom gone? No, not gone, but where does it reside? That's the location we must seek and hopefully find. And when we do, we will know the past, sense the people of the past, know their knowledge, their lore, their thoughts, their beliefs." PB paused, releasing Sara's hand. "That's what I do for people like your mother who are willing to believe in the practice." She thought for a moment and then added with emphasis, "To believe otherwise runs contrary to the great beyond that is human hope."

Sara's mother was growing impatient. After what Sara observed were restless, anxious moments of silence, her mother whispered and then repeated in a stronger emotional tone, "Mr. Knox! Mr. Knox? I'm here. Your daughter is here."

PB repeated the summons, slowly, emphasizing his last name. Her voice changed, now deeper, contralto, becoming masculine, Sara thought.

More silence. Mother said softly, "It is snowing hard, Mr. Knox. But the ambulance is coming." She added, "Soon, soon…" and her voice drifted off as silence filled the room."

Sara watched one of the candles flicker and continue to do so. PB gestured toward it and whispered in a hint of recognition, "Mr. Knox!"

Intently Sara watched the candle flame as she inhaled the alluring scents. From somewhere, she heard the word, "pain."

Her mother began to weep softly. PB said, "Is your pain bad, Mr. Knox?" She added, "Yes, of course it is."

Her mother said, "My poor father. Where is our ambulance?"

Spellbound, Sara said softly, "Grandfather?"

"He doesn't know you," Sara's mother said, almost in a reprimand. "You weren't born yet."

PB whispered, "Mother, he does know your daughter."

Another candle flickered.

Sara looked into the flame. Slowly the flame became a face, a nod perhaps, a smile surely, a male voice, a deep word, or was it a suggestion of recognition? Was it her grandfather? Sara was sure it was. She was certain she was sensing the past. She felt she could see into the deepness of its people. Dare she acknowledge her experience? Dare she relate this day to any of her high school classmates?

CHAPTER SIX:
THE IDEA FOR HER FUTURE

Sara snapped out of it and brought herself back to the present. Embarrassed, Kinkaid eased his body away from her. Sara's thoughts shifted back to herself and her future. She wished she could forget Kinkaid and simply get on with graduation and celebrate the commencement of the rest of her life along with Manny, who regrettably no longer was holding her hand. First, she would work to earn her doctorate in history. Then she'd hope to get a job? Yes, she needed a job. Without a job, how ever was she to repay her student loans? Here in what everyone was saying was economically depressed southern Indiana, there were few jobs and, for sure, none at a closed college in a geographically bypassed part of the American dream. Where was, and what was her future to be?

To answer herself, Sara acknowledged she must listen to Kinkaid and consider his plan if for no reason other than her innate curiosity about men—this older man in particular—who was old enough to be her father. But what about life—her own young life—given her uncertain life ahead? With history and its exploration off somewhere in her future—yes, that's what she yearned for—an answer, a direction, a calling, some sort of certainty. But how and where was it to be found? Kinkaid's special project seemed a possibility. And what if it were? Was it a fit for her?

*   *   *

Later that day, at Kinkaid's invitation, Sara returned to the professor's idiosyncratic office. She hadn't decided if it was his weird desk or its gold ingot that induced the allure of a rich challenge that lay beyond. After class, Manny had told her in a commanding voice, which she resisted, not to go, not to look into Kinkaid's research project, but instead to accompany him and the other students to the party at the student union before it, too, was shut down for good. She told Manny that during this graduation week she'd had enough alcohol. Now, this day, this evening, was her private time to get serious about graduate school and the rest of her life. Besides, she was interested to see what their professor might offer. "Why not go?" she said to Manny. "By nature we historians are curious."

For sure, she worried that graduation would cut her off from college friends as they dispersed, moving on to explore the next phase of their lives. Even her own young man was focusing on his tomorrow in a graduate program devoted to mining and minerals. Kyra had confided her plan to go back to Indianapolis and marry into a particular young man's family—an event her roommate talked about more and more as she formulated romantic plans for an idyllic married life—children, a stately house, the right cars, a five-bedroom cabin hugging the shore of Lake Tippecanoe. They would attend the prestigious Memorial Day Speedway time trials and the ensuing 500-Mile Race watching from his family's private box and talking to and idolizing the Hollywood and political celebrities who would be invited to join them as they orbited in their universe of prestige. And then there would be the pro football stadium boxes in the big indoor coliseum. For her, it was to be success by association, as Sara commented, only in return to receive a scowl, perhaps a frown of fear from Kyra that Sara's evaluation might be right on. Nevertheless, the two women vowed to stay in touch and continue their collegiate friendship.

CHAPTER SEVEN:
ERIKA WOLFE

Outside the door of Kinkaid's office, after a fleeting moment of concern as to the direction of her life, Sara took courage and entered. To her surprise, she saw an unknown woman hugging and kissing Professor Kinkaid. She was attractive in a stylish yet mature manner with appropriate attire enhanced by likely valuable jewelry displayed in appropriately placed adornments. To herself, Sara decried her own miniscule collection of jewelry, comparing it with this woman's and even Kyra's. On campus, thinking cosmetically, Sara had allied herself to Professor Morris, who, like her, was focused on the halls of academia, not on female appearance. Like her, Sara wore no nail polish; she had no necklace; she had not braided her hair, or tied a bow in it. She had become so engrossed in her studies that she had overlooked her appearance. And as she took on the task of her dissertation, it would likely continue that way. Yet she had a pink cell phone cover and often wore pink shoes. Wasn't that enough, along with her proclaimed academic intent, to indicate gender loyalty?

Sara wondered what she might look like in her old age, but then this woman wasn't exactly "old age." What was "old age" anyway? Kinkaid? Her own father? It had been so long since she had seen her father, she didn't know whether to classify him as "old, really old, or not that old."

As for this well-attired and stately woman embracing Kinkaid, it seemed more her doing than his, though he was clearly a willing participant in the entwining of bodies. Sara coughed, announcing her arrival. Their canoodling continued for a moment, but then ended, their contented expressions lingering, their arms reluctantly lowering. Behind them on his desk, Sara saw a half-empty bottle of wine and wineglasses, one with lipstick.

What is it with age? Is it consuming too much alcohol? For

Kinkaid, perhaps it is pain from sciatica—whatever that ailment is. Or is it lament or even sadness over their earlier or even present lives that is muddling their minds, mitigated by alcohol? But why? How old are these two older people? She is not as old as he. Sara wondered if being young is so different from these two older people. Well, it obviously is. They have had, or the woman may still have her career, while she, Sara, was hoping to embark on her own. Yet Kinkaid's career was over, along with James Whitcomb Riley College. When does an afterlife begin? For Kinkaid? For the college? And what if there is none for either? Sara wondered about this duo. Overriding, loomed her own future.

"Sara," welcomed Kinkaid, his arm extending toward his student as he offered his handshake, not, she felt, as teacher to student, but at this moment, so she speculated, as one colleague to another. Was it a shift to her being recognized—for wasn't she about to become an alum going on to becoming a doctoral candidate, officially degreed by sheepskin—at least by an accredited American college?

Kinkaid said, "Sara, I'd like you to meet Dr. Erika Wolfe. She's on the board—actually one of the founders—of the Institute to End War, or IEW in Geneva."

The visiting PhD said, "Ms. Vogel, nice to meet you. Professor Kinkaid speaks highly of you." The older woman sipped her wine and smiled, either from the drink or out of politeness. Sara was unsure which. She returned the smile automatically without specific meaning on her part. In surprise, she heard herself ask, "He does speak of me?" And wondered why she said that.

Dr. Wolfe said, "Oh, yes, and most favorably."

"Dr. Wolfe runs a think tank," Kinkaid said. "Isn't that right, Erika?"

"I think so," she said and laughed.

"Ending war is a lot to think about." Sara said. She came up short for she was soon to become an American university graduate, and she'd been taught not to end a sentence with a preposition. So she quickly added, "What I meant to say is, "That is a huge issue."

Dr. Wolfe said, "It is. That's why we need the help of Professor Kinkaid. You'll be pleased to know that my Institute to End War is offering your president a position in our Geneva office... that is, after his college—this college—shuts down. Once there, he'll be thinking in tandem with the rest of us."

"Nice," Sara said and smiled at Kinkaid, who nodded with evident pleasure. "And what will you do, Sir, in Geneva in this new academic beyond? What will each of you be thinking about?" Uh, oh, she'd done it again. Correcting, she said, "I mean, about what will you—all of you—be thinking?"

Erika said in a rather rehearsed fashion, so Sara surmised, "Our mission is to study war and especially why we humans fight so many wars." She sounded as if she had said this many times. She added. "Your professor will help us research why wars start, how they're financed, and how to prevent them. Complex stuff but important."

Sara thought Dr. Erika Wolfe was okay, eschewing academic vocabulary to use the word "stuff." Sara recalled that Professor Kinkaid wasn't a PhD himself. She hadn't paid much attention to JWR instructors' academic credentials, the sequence of letters following their name. What she cared about was whether the course was significant. Then she focused on completing assignments, passing tests, earning good grades, keeping up her grade point average; getting her degree. Now she had new goals, especially preparing for a career. And perhaps marriage and maybe someday a baby, and with some luck, career success. A full life. The fact that Professor Kinkaid had only a master's degree hadn't kept students from admiring him, learning, and benefiting from attending his classes.

*   *   *

Accepting the professor's offer of a glass of wine, Sara recalled his telling her why he hadn't written the dissertation and passed the oral exams to earn the coveted PhD degree, allowing him to advance into the ranks of elite academicians.

That day she had said to her mentor, "You're a great teacher. You think about us, your students. You guide us. Don't colleges covet faculty members who do that?"

He had replied, "Yes, of course. But you asked for the reason I didn't go on to get my doctorate." To her nod, he had said, "You see, I was well along in the pursuit of my graduate degree in history at the big state university up in Bloomington. But as luck would have it, I ran afoul of the head of the department. He was overseeing my research on the question of why we in Western Civilization have fought so many wars. It was an area he had spent his life studying. I was beginning to focus on how wars are financed and by whom, which is a narrower topic. Yet my question is vital to understanding the reasons for war."

As an aside, Kincaid had said to her, "In my opinion, few historians understand finance. For them, money is an amorphous abstraction... like those enigmatic black holes we read about in outer space. No one knows for sure what's inside, or how to tame such unknowns. Most historians are afraid to explore, afraid if they reveal their lack of understanding about finance they'll appear uninformed to their students and faculty."

Sara had nodded. "True, there's not much interest in the workings of finance among my campus friends."

"Nor from war buffs, either," Kinkaid had said. "All they want to talk about is weapon superiority, famous battles, crowd-rousing speeches, charismatic leaders—each important, of course. But, Sara, without wars being financed, none of those subjects would be there to research, to study, lecture about, and write books that readers will buy. In my opinion, the ramifications of finance are key to why and how wars are launched, carried out, and maybe someday ended."

Kinkaid went on: "In high school, my history teacher said that every organization—whether corporate, nonprofit, or university—is run by and for the benefit of the people running it. The same is true of wars—they're run by and for the benefit of the people starting them and trying to run them: the politicians, the bankers, the financiers, the generals."

She had prodded. "Did something happen between you and your dean?"

"Indeed it did! The dean—his name was Merlin Ellis—was known and respected by scholars and students. As if worshiping a cult leader, they obediently bought into his professed reason behind every war."

"Which was?"

To her surprise, Kinkaid snorted, a non-verbal expression she hadn't heard and then said, "Ellis hypothesized that wars are ideologically inspired by manipulative rulers pursuing their own agenda. Then, so cajoled, regular people dutifully fight these wars for these ideological reasons, following the causes their leader has extolled. The soldiers have become convinced to kill and even die for the ruler's cause. In his books, Ellis cited example after example, going back to the Greeks, the Romans—plunder and rape satisfying their leader's nationalist, ethnic, or religious ideology. He was fond of citing the World War I Turks' Gatling gun stand at Gallipoli. They were following the rallying cry of the general who became known as Ataturk. He inspired his countrymen to fight and die. Vikings promised plunder and riches in response to the rallying commands of their leaders. The Crusades were inspired by religious leaders advancing their personal holy cause, which they camouflaged to say was for the benefit of "The Church." You get the picture, his picture, Ellis's picture."

She recalled going along with her professor.

"One dared not take issue with Merlin Ellis, PhD, certainly not one of his students. I think he feared that I could sooner or later be in a position to challenge his reputation. He began to criticize my research and denigrate my opinions—all of which, in his mind, ran contrary to his years of being an authority among historians on the cause of war."

"What did you do?"

"In my studies delving into history, I came to disagree professionally with the theories advocated by him in his books and publications. I became convinced of my own views about the need for accumulating more money, more gold, as being the cause of war. I was the lone academic contradicting Ellis' reputation. He grew hostile toward me."

"What happened?"

"It became apparent that he was never going to approve my proposal for my dissertation. As a result, I was not going to receive my PhD. Worse, I concluded, he was going to expel me from his history department. My advocacy in favor of my own theory represented a diatribe against him—or that's how he took it. All this venom occurred without a chance for us to have a conversation. With us being in the same institution of higher learning, my belief that war is caused by the quest for riches, for money, and not ideological reasons, served only to question his life's work and potentially discredit his writings and lectures. I was a threat to his legacy.

"One tense day in class, with our differences becoming apparent in front of students, Ellis and I exchanged abrasive heated words. In a burst of temper-driven rage, he informed me and everyone in class that I was no longer welcome in his history department. Given his verbal trigger to my emotions, he and I began swearing at each other. Sara, my whole life—what I had seen myself as becoming, a PhD faculty member of a university history department—suddenly those dreams were going down the drain. I was in a no man's land of confusion, disappointment and, yes, frustration. He—an icon in the field of history—was expelling me from the world of studying, writing, and teaching in my chosen field.

"In anger—wanton rage it was—I threw an eraser at him while students looked on in a combination of horror and, I suppose, amusement. And then, my rage boiling, I picked up a chair, and it followed the trajectory of the eraser, each in succession, and to forever to my regret, hitting Dean Ellis broadside."

Sara had gulped. "An eraser and then... a chair! But, Sir, didn't you think, didn't you realize? I mean, you were killing your career..."

"When I enrolled in his department, I took him as a real friend, a mentor, more than a dean guiding an aspiring PhD student. My disappointment in him, in my situation, and in myself, ran rampant. I was out of control with anger."

Sara had nodded, hoping to learn more.

Kinkaid said, "The Korean War was raging. The draft was on. Ellis promptly annulled my deferment. When I tried to transfer to other colleges to pursue my thesis and my degree, he badmouthed me. He was so respected in his field that they listened to him. Re-classified as 1-A, I was called to duty. After basic training, I was sent to Korea. Now I ask you: in 1950, where and what was the ideology to justify that savage war?"

Sara had said, "I suppose property. Communists would take property away from the Capitalists." After his acknowledging smile, she went on, "But you survived the war and after that made your way in academic circles."

"Yes. In the war, with my history background, I managed to get an assignment to a select intelligence unit whose mission was to trace how the Chinese and Russians were funding their Communist allies in North Korea. Our unit discovered that the Reds were getting their money through established international banking circles."

"That knowledge fortified your beliefs about how wars are financed?"

"Yes, it did, but while we were finding out how the North Koreans were paying for weapons, troops, bombs, airplane fuel, and tanks, thousands of American soldiers and pilots—apart from the Koreans, Chinese, and our allies—were being killed, wounded, and captured on the battlefield. I mean, just in the Battle of Pork Chop Hill, thousands of young American men were killed in order to capture some damn little mountain. Today, there are still soldiers missing in action from that war."

Kinkaid continued, "Think, Sara, for a minute about the many lives that were destroyed, families devastated, human beings— American men, no, really boys, were killed, never to become husbands or fathers, never to contribute their ideas or their creativity to society, never to raise children, never to live the American dream. That is what war does to a culture. It devastates."

Sara suggested, "But you went on? Those experiences made you want to learn more about financing wars."

"It did. After the Korean ceasefire, I came home and married my college sweetheart. My dear wife's father was an alum of Riley College. He helped me get my faculty appointment. The Board and faculty overlooked my lack of a PhD. Over time, I built a reputation as an exceptional teacher. Eventually, against all odds, I became college president. Which left me no time to pursue my true passion. So, now..."

She wondered out loud, "Where was your dean's compassion?"

"Rigidity of beliefs trumps empathy and compassion." Kinkaid asked, "Why is it that in our culture we feel compelled to judge each other? We instinctively form up or down opinions about those with whom we come in contact. Is it that way with you young people, too? Has nothing changed for the better in generational traits over the years?"

Sara didn't want to judge her college president, her boyfriend Manny, or her roommate Kyra, and certainly not her mother who, on her own, had raised her. Nor did she want to judge her enigmatic and distant father, although given his lack of participation in her life, he seemed at fatherly fault. Perhaps he had his reasons, his own life to live.

Sara thought further and replied to her professor, "I think my generation is more tolerant, more open-minded, more compassionate about the differences in people. Maybe that's what has changed in our regard for others."

Kinkaid seemed pleased and smiled, so Sara thought, a smile of hope. She had asked, "Where is Dean Ellis now, these many years later?"

"Maybe lost in the archival heaven of library stacks, where so many academics go for seclusion and from having to deal with the real world." He added, "As for me, I want to stay in the real world—which is the nuts and bolts of financing wars. All these years later, as you saw from my pleadings today to my students—especially to you, Sara—I want someone to rally to the cause and pursue what I consider to be my important World War II research project."

Sara realized he hadn't answered her question, so she let the matter drop, only to hear him say in a pining tone, "Maybe someday Ellis and I will reconcile. You know, I hope so, for I disdain on-going hate." From that day on, she regarded Kinkaid as her friend. She felt they enjoyed a rapport that spanned the difference in age.

CHAPTER EIGHT:
LOOKING FORWARD

N ow, in the presence of Kinkaid and Dr. Wolfe, concern for her professor caused her to ask, "Will you find opportunity in Geneva and comfort?"

Dr. Wolfe smiled at Kinkaid and replied. "It's his chance to make up for having been cheated out of his PhD degree. Ms. Vogel, this project of his is a perfect topic for a dissertation. Choosing to pursue it will help you earn your doctorate. Launch your career, too" She gestured at Sara and said to Kinkaid, "She can pursue the seminal ideas you were developing under Dean Ellis."

Sensing Sara's interest growing, Kinkaid said, "Sara, here's what we want you to do, and you can do it with aplomb. Please write a research proposal. It'll get us started toward accomplishing a mutual goal."

"Sounds like an assignment." Sara's enthusiasm rose as she saw the responsive nods and smiles from each. She went on, "I recall the proposal I submitted for my senior thesis, Professor Kinkaid, to compare the party platforms of the two U. S. political parties at their national conventions throughout the 20th century. That was a real challenge—"

"—Sara, this proposal is much different—"

"—Took four weeks, or more, as I recall."

"This proposal is shorter. Assuming you want to work with us at IEW, the next step is for you to submit a concise proposal to Erika. She needs it to justify to the Institute's Board of Directors the stipend covering your compensation and expenses. "You can write it as quickly as your last exam at JWR."

Erika said, "Yes, it's a proposal for the task you will be undertaking."

Sara was puzzled. "And that, more precisely, is?"

Kinkaid said, "It's a chance of a lifetime, Sara. You'll travel to

Switzerland and conduct research in a medieval chateau. You'll be looking into events that took place there during World War II."

Sara smiled. "I'm getting excited."

Kincaid went on, "A group of central bankers representing the warring parties lived and worked there."

"While the war was going on everywhere else?"

They both nodded.

Erika said, "For your dissertation, which I promise you IEW will approve, you will delve into the events that took place. Your objective will be to define how this clandestine group of rogue bankers financed the war. It's a topic right up your history alley, as well as the banking career of your father."

"My father?"

"Yes," Erika said. "His Bank for International Settlements—not the BIS of today, but instead, its role during World War II."

"But he wasn't even born then, I don't think.

"Kinkaid said, "He knows what took place."

Sara reflected, "I suppose he would know about that time."

"I assure you he does," Erika said.

"Yes, but even with a PhD degree, no one will pay heed to me."

Kinkaid looked at Sara. "What you will have to say in your dissertation and then in your book, I guarantee, will be of note to everyone. Rest assured, today the world is taking young women seriously, reporting what they say, and what they write." Gesturing to Erika, he added in an embarrassed tone, "Older women, too." Back to Sara, he said, "With Erika's think tank sponsoring you, given your forthcoming scholarly credentials, having IEW publish your book will prove most supportive."

Switzerland, a Medieval chateau. A book, Sara fantasized. Her own history book. Wow! She couldn't believe it, yet she was warming to these two older people and to their plan to include her. She asked, "What exactly is it I'm to be researching? I mean, toward what objective am I headed in my studies? What conclusions will I be seeking? What do I need to do to earn an A Plus?" She laughed as if back at JWR.

Erika's quick response told her, "Simply do your job. Your writing is to be your voice—your own words on the subject of war and how World War II was financed. You will be reporting to the world about what you learn from being inside this historic Swiss chateau. And what you may find in the little town of Rougemont."

Before Sara could reply, Dr. Wolfe changed the subject, asking, "By the way, your professor has told me about your name change. Out of curiosity, I must ask you why your parents never informed you of your royal family legacy?"

Sara recoiled, not wanting to answer. Why was she being asked? She wanted to blurt abruptly—closing off the unwelcome subject of parents—"My parents are dead." But she couldn't say that because they knew it wasn't true, although, as far as she was concerned, her father might as well be. And her mother was, well, out of touch with familial life, lost in her spirit world. Instead, she said, "Why do my parents matter?" Then wished she'd just stated that they weren't very involved in her life, hoping such a closeout would put an end to Dr. Wolfe's query.

Face it: her mother was lost in her own weird way searching for contact with one or more of her ancestors and had not shared much about family other than the desire to somehow talk to her deceased father. As to her father, he had briefly acknowledged secrets off in the dark past, with maybe blanks to be filled in, as if in his life their Vogel family story was as unimportant as an unwanted child. Only hints were allowed to linger about something that someday might be disclosed. And that had been that. And so, the subject of family history had faded from her mind.

Except for her brother Jack, who last summer... Sara choked up. Tears came. Last summer. She saw the image of her beloved brother before he had gone off to the Afganistan for his third tour of duty where he'd stepped on a mine and blown himself up into patriotic soldier heaven. Wherever that was. She relived the flag-folding final tribute, with the honor guard's guns sounding. Yes, it was Jack who had alerted her that there was more to their family heritage. It was that wonderful time when she was so happy to have him home on leave. Her older brother, now dead in some far-off war devoid of causes other than the protection of property of the wealthy, digging for and refining oil—material values essential for the continued growth of Western economies. Well, it wasn't really a war, was it? What was it called, anyway? What difference did a label make? It was only a description for death and destruction. And, she added, precious black gold.

Bother Jack had been killed. War was war. But what was war? Any situation in which people were killing each other was a war. Was Dr. Wolfe's think tank concerned about fighting these smaller wars, or were she and IEW against all fighting, all violence, toward women, children, even toward men?

All Sara could think about at that moment was what she imagined Kinkaid, and now Dr. Wolfe, and soon herself might do to pursue and then validate her research and her resultant writing. She was going to look into war and how the killing was paid for. In some chateau in Switzerland. Sara envisioned her brother's last moment, his fateful step detonating the landmine. Maybe she owed it to Jack to take on this research project. But to find out about war? About finance? She, Sara Vogel. She, Sara von Reichard. She, a novice, yet a researcher, working on her own PhD dissertation.

But she was as green as unmown Indiana hay. Who would pay any heed to what she discovered, wrote about, and published? Why, when academics before her had ignored Kinkaid, or had they? If they had gone to battlefields, interviewed male leaders, marched with male armies, saluted male generals, why had they not gone where Kinkaid wanted to go? Was it because they didn't understand finance?

But what if there was a story here that no one else had covered? A story that few know about. That Kinkaid and now she—Sara Vogel nee von Reichard—was on to? Maybe the finance story she was to research would reveal women in this bit of history and not, as was usually the case, just men.

CHAPTER NINE:
THE PREVIOUS SUMMER

S ara recalled that it had been up at their ever-so-familiar vacation lake in the northern part of the state. Almost a year ago now— late last summer—right after Labor Day. School had started, and most of the late summer vacationers had departed for home. She and brother Jack were sitting on a pair of Adirondack chairs on the sloping lawn separating the historic wooden lodge from the lakeshore. The air was Hoosier humid and, of course, perspiration hot—a typical Indiana late summer afternoon. Jack had one final day of leave before going back to the other side of the world to re-join his Army unit. She remembered treasuring this precious day with her big brother. He resembled, she thought, more their father than their mother. Whom did she resemble? Their father, too, she hoped. But why did she feel that way?

Jack had lingered, not wanting to go with her for a walk around the lake on the familiar path they used to enjoy taking together. Perhaps in his reluctance, he was trying to deny that within days he would be back in Afghanistan and possibly in some military skirmish or combat. She remembered he had looked at her and said, "Why can't we simply hold on to this present moment here in each other's company? Lock it in—if not forever, at least for long enough to savor, to examine, to paint on a canvas, write about on a laptop, or photographs on our cell phones?" Lamenting, he had added in a tone she had rarely heard, "Sara... Sis... our precious moments together have been few and far between. I don't want our time together today to end."

Comfortable in this exceptional moment of having Jack by her side, Sara relished their long overdue brother-sister camaraderie. Such togetherness had been rare in their sibling years. Jack, so it seemed, was always doing something different, going off to school, or to somewhere to run in one of his marathons or ironman races. He traveled a lot, somehow chasing after the world at top speed. Meanwhile she stayed home, studying, reading, and living the young life of Indianapolis with her girlfriends and occasionally boys.

She recalled past summer vacations—precious moments surveying the lake, taking in the surrounding deciduous forests waiting to turn into the Fall season while treasuring the historic lodge. There had been several—actually more than a few—cute boyfriends with their many attempts to kiss her, their few treasured successes, she swimming out to the old wooden platform with its inflated green plastic mermaid. After lounging there like the other teen-agers, splashing everyone, she would swim back in, the beautiful bodies of the boys... the excited chatter of the girls. As she advanced the timeframe of memories, she recalled how her friends had each moved on in age and thought. They had begun to voice their plans—or maybe no plans at all in some cases—for college, jobs, perhaps even marriage. Life, her life and theirs, continued to advance like pieces on a multi-tiered chessboard of time.

She remembered replying to Jack, "Time passes. We move on with the calendar. We can't help it. We are irrevocably tuned to the trumpet of time."

He had grasped her hand and said, "Then, Sis, it's time for me—before I go back—to tell you what I have found out about our family and our ancestors."

Surprised, yet curious, she had asked, "What, Jack?"

"I'm assigned to G-2—that's Military Intelligence. And it's not an oxymoron, it's real stuff. I've a 'Top Secret' clearance with access to all sorts of information. I've been vetted by the FBI." He paused and, more serious, said, "I've thought about the future. This time I may not come back, or I may be wounded and not able to remember the information. Let me tell you while it's fresh in my mind."

Sara had waited. She always waited for Jack, for he was her older brother, and older brothers always took the lead while sisters waited. That was the way society was programmed. Women—most women—sat back and waited. Wasn't that the way families worked? Like the father always took the lead. Like that? You know! Right? She told herself again that history has always been written that way. And she renewed her vow to break new ground in her career.

Jack had begun, "It seems that our grandfather in Germany thought he might be part Jewish, feared it actually. In 1935, after the

Nazis passed the anti-Semitic Nuremburg Laws, every German family was required to research their genealogy and complete a family lineage chart. If you reported you were Jewish, or even partly so—and they had ways they could verify the accuracy of your data—you could be picked up, even on suspicion of being Jewish, and hauled off to a camp. Maybe never to return, maybe soon to be dead."

Sara said, "How awful."

"Our grandfather's family name was von Reichard. He feared showing up as part Jewish—you see, he believed his grandfather's mother—our ancestor—was Jewish from a community in eastern Germany. Hoping to cover this up, he changed our family name, and chose Vogel, or "bird" in English—perhaps to characterize his anticipated flight from the Fatherland to escape the danger he feared."

"He wanted the name to sound Aryan?"

"A lot of Germans did the same thing. Jewish sounding names were changed, all the while trying to conceal what might be construed as that ethnic line, even if they were only a quarter Jewish, or didn't really know. People were scared."

They heard thunder as dark clouds began to blow across the late afternoon sky. Jack had looked up, pointed, and said, "Floating southeast off the Great Lakes. Timely. They're bringing a hint of Fall. Halloween, The Goblins'll get you if you don't watch out. The fragrance of new mown hay, the fodder's in the shock, the frost is on the pumpkin, and overhead the bright harvest moon with its reflection off the Wabash. Sara, I hate to leave Indiana this time of year."

Not hesitating, she said, "Then don't."

Jack went on, "Our grandfather and his father were related to German royalty—as are we. We go back to one of the ancient German principalities, Hesse-Kassel, with its ruling dynasty of princes and princesses. Some of them had a Jewish line. There was little or no problem, long ago, living in German principalities and being Jewish. In hindsight, in comparison with the early 20th century, for the most part, people lived in harmony."

"But royalty? Our family?"

"World War II pretty well did away with the significance of German royalty. Many royals were killed fighting in the war. Others had their estates confiscated, usually by the Russians setting up the new East German state behind the Iron Curtain. Yet the lineages remain. Just not much talked about, except among those who are actually related to royalty. They know who they are and stay in touch."

"But not in touch with us?"

Jack was silent.

"There's more to the 1930's story?"

"Yes. In fear, our grandfather fled Germany."

"From where? What was his trade, his background?"

"He was a banker. For years, maybe centuries, our family lived in the ancient village of Mockmuhl near Stuttgart. Dates back to AD 771."

"That's really old! But where did grandfather go?"

"Switzerland. To the Swiss Alps near Gstaad. To Chateau D/Ox. There, he thought, he would be safe and where in nearby Rougemont, so I suppose, he might have been offered a job from a German royal who had already gotten out of Germany. That last part is speculation."

Rain began to fall, and they sought shelter inside the lodge. There, she looked up at her brother and said in what she hoped was a loving sisterly tone, "Jack, dearest, why are you going back? Why? Why don't you quit the army and get a real job somewhere around here— in the U.S., that is, I mean, and not put your life on the line—every day—in some faraway meaningless place?"

Before returning to the family's traditional lake cabin and packing for the return trip to their parents' house where Jack would say goodbye to his mother and to her once again, he replied to his sister, "I must. It is my duty."

"To whom? To what?"

"To myself, I guess."

"Certainly not to me."

"Yes, to you, as well, more than anyone else, Sara."

"But to our mother? And to our father?"

"Yes, to them, to both. To all of you." He seemed pleased with his answer but not with the look from Sara.

Slowly she said to her older brother, "My professor—"

"—Some impractical academic..."

"—President of the college and a historian."

"Did he ever serve?"

"To fight?"

"Yes, in combat."

"Yes, in Korea—"

"—Well, what does he have to say about war?"

"This past year we've read a lot of books and papers about war, going back to the Athenian hoplites and the Romans." She saw Jack fidget. "Hear me out," she insisted.

"I'm sorry, Sis. Please go on."

"My professor is intense, dedicated to his subject and to his students."

"Including you?"

Pleased, she smiled and went on, "Ever since the Battle of Marathon, wars have gotten more awful as weaponry advanced from spears to nuclear bombs. Some day we'll all be wiped out by some bomb, chemical, or germ. There's no logic to any of it." Her voice rose. "War is just plain wrong!"

"I don't disagree with your conclusion."

"This semester we're going to read Chris Hedges' *War is the Source that Gives Life Meaning*."

"Well, Sis, be assured that my life has meaning, a dedicated cause."

"Really? Tell me what it is."

Jack looked annoyed. "Democracy, of course. It's what our leaders, our generals, tell us is our mission. It's what you might call a generational goal, begun with those who fought in The Great War. Then, in World War II, it's what 'The Greatest Generation' fought for. Today, many in my generation subscribe to the popular idea that it's our duty to bring democracy to the rest of the world. Ask anyone in the Service today."

Sara sensed she should agree, but had difficulty doing so. She simply nodded, recognizing her brother and the dangerous path he had chosen.

CHAPTER TEN:
THE OLD HOME PLACE

D riving back to Indianapolis and observing the flat Indiana farmlands—the ubiquitous fields of row after row of corn alternating with fields of waving wheat, each crop nearing its fall harvest—with Jack at the wheel, of course, Sara talked openly about their parents. She explored her feelings about her mother and her seldom-present father. Jack's presence reminded her that they were each progeny of a mother-father team, a parent couple, a two-some. Briefly, she speculated as to what it must have been like for the two of them before "we two siblings" were born.

"No way for me to know," Jack said. "I don't recall their ever talking about much of anything." He drove on in silence, finally saying, "Exercise became my idea of conversation." Passing more fields, he added, "I seldom heard either of them converse."

She knew that her father, following the career pattern of his father before him, was a banker. In her recollections, his financial role had been played only for a brief time in their hometown. Soon, Sara recalled, he was no longer making loans to businesses or mortgages to homeowners. Instead, in what he had said was a career advancement, he became a staff member of the Federal Reserve Bank up north in Chicago. It was one of the twelve regional banks that made up America's central bank, the Federal Reserve System, divided as it was—so her father had explained quickly to her the one time when she asked—into 12 geographic districts across the country. In another of their infrequent conversations, her father made sure she understood the bank was voted into existence by Congress way back in 1913.

"Why not sooner?" she had asked.

She didn't like the look he had given her—impatience mixed with rudeness—not a father's thoughtful explanation. "People, and I include Congressmen, back then and still today, don't much understand money." His gruff reply, softened a bit, went on, "But after so many financial panics over the years, enough people said something should be done to manage the national economy better and control its money supply in order to protect banks and businesses from failing."

And that was that—the sum total of her banking education. Most of the time, when she did see him on one of his infrequent two-day visits, it seemed he was getting on the train at the Union Station right away and going back to Chicago or, later in her life, flying off in one of the bank's private jets. He spent so much time in Chicago that she worried he had, in reality, deserted their family. Then one day, her mother told her that he had gone to Switzerland, to Basel, to work at some place called the Bank for International Settlements. "What do they do there?" she had asked.

"Something to do with countries' central banks and their stacks of gold bars." Her mother had seemed as uninterested in the topic as much as she appeared to be in her husband and maybe, Sara worried, life in general. No more meaningful information was forthcoming, so Sara put banking out of her mind. She also wanted to put her father out of her mind. Yet he remained an opaque image in a corner of her thoughts.

In conversations with her fellow students, banking was never discussed, other than maybe what to do about an expired ATM card. Or maybe, did a parent go to the bank and send money? Seldom were fathers mentioned. In Sara's case, as far as she knew, her father was in Basel, a major Swiss city she had found on the Internet, contiguous to both Germany and France.

Her mother had seemed to endure her husband's absence, not with a growing loneliness, but rather a done-deal life-lost attitude. Given her obsession with trying, through episodes with one clairvoyant after another, to make contact with her own deceased father, she had taken on an emotional aloofness from real life, a denial, Sara thought, of her marital situation. That left Sara doubting her mother's acceptance of reality. And maybe even her sanity. On the other hand, her mother had sort of always been there for Sara, so it had seemed during her growing up, to answer questions and on rare occasions to talk about things that mattered to a growing daughter.

Meanwhile, during her upbringing, Jack often left home to follow his own life pursuits and especially his scheduled athletic events. She had become self-reliant, disciplining herself in her day-to-day life. She had come to regard herself as a self-supporting and mature young woman, ready for life's adventures.

Sara thought about the attitudes of her fellow students who, from time to time, complained that parents were part of their growing-up problems—either too distant and uninterested, or too close, hovering over them and trying to micro-manage their lives. Such opinions surfaced when they'd had a few beers at the student union, or when they were depressed about their studies or experiencing difficulties in their social lives, or when they were high on the drug du-jour. Or when... oh shit, why did she have to go down that dead-end road?

She watched a farmer's tractor maneuver along rows of corn as it harvested the ears. She wondered what it would be like to farm the land of Indiana. She contemplated the rural life as the countryside passed like frames in a movie. She visualized herself living as a farm wife, gathering eggs from the chickens in the coop, milking the cows in the barn, canning the fruit picked from a small orchard, and helping to give birth to little lambs and even calves, and herself giving birth to a platoon of farm workers. "No," she told herself, "that's not going to be my life!"

In the car that day, Sara had really wanted to think about the days and months ahead—for now was her time to review her future. Maybe she was looking at better days than her parents hoped for and planned back when they were her age. Or maybe not. They'd had it easy. His job, a car, a house. Or was life that easy for them? They had never talked about their own lives.

Sara had to admit that she hadn't asked her parents about their lives. Their conversations were more about her or her brother, their school, studies, clothes, cars, dates—that is, when there were conversations. Parents certainly talked among themselves, privately. Maybe it was pillow talk—or with other couples, maybe little or no talk at all—she didn't know. She seldom, if ever, asked her mother questions about the guidelines that had charted her life. She basically let the past—their parents' past—remain back there in the past, the distant out-of-sight past, the maybe I-don't-really-care-that-much past.

She tried once more, querying Jack, "What do you make of our father?"

"Lance? That's his name. I called him that whenever I talked to him, which was seldom, too seldom for real father-son talk. He's strange." Jack reflected, "Being in the intelligence service, I've seen a lot of unusual fellows. I mean, basic weirdoes. Our father might fit that definition, but instead he's in banking, and bankers, so I've always hoped, are not weirdoes. He's got some strange ideas, though—the few times we've talked."

"About what?"

"War. Gold. And his bank's role in both." Jack paused. "Like, you know, what's important in life—the force above all else."

"Which is?"

"Gold. Every conversation eventually comes around to money, to gold, as if it were our religion to worship the mineral."

Sara realized they had entered Indianapolis and were driving along their street, Central Avenue. Familiar territory from her youthful years. With some apprehension, she watched the houses float past, revisiting a series of unpleasant memories, but also pleasant ones, each from high school or before. Then they were there. Jack steered the car into their family driveway and parked in front of the single garage door.

Seeing her childhood home again brought back more specific memories. She was a little girl on a hot Hoosier day playing in the lawn sprinkler, but with no father watching, only a mother coming later and carrying an outstretched towel. And then she was off to her own room to put on her little jump suit. Sara remembered her bed, her desk, her closet, her precious dolls, her animals. Stuffed, not real. What had been real? Her growing up. About to part from her brother and to leave her old home, Sara realized she was grown up, at least she felt so with only one year of college remaining. After that, she hoped for graduate school.

She yearned to sneak a visit to her old bedroom. She did, going behind the garage to her once private door. Except now there was no door, only strings of beads hanging from the lintel. She brushed them aside. Looking inside, she saw nothing familiar, only weird posters of clairvoyants amid pictures of moons and stars. Other strange devices covered the walls. In disbelief, Sara turned and fled back to the car and Jack. Her room, she told herself—no longer her room—had moved on to a college campus in the southern part of the state. After graduation, it was due to move again. Whatever and wherever that might turn out to be…

Earlier in the car, Jack had continued their brother-sister conversation, "Someday I'd like to grill Lance in the same way we interrogate terrorists we capture."

"Jack! He's our father!"

"Lance is not terribly human. We get that trait from our ancestors—skips a generation, I say." Jack mused for a moment and said, "There was this incident. I've never told anyone."

"Tell me now."

Jack looked at Sara and nodded. "I was in Chicago to run the marathon—"

"—A full marathon, of course."

"Yes. Twenty-six miles plus two hundred and eighty-five yards. After I had crossed the finish line and refueled my body with a beer and the usual goodies, Lance took me to meet the Governor—not of the state, but the head man in our Federal Reserve District."

"Did he have a big office?"

Jack nodded, "A high rise inside the Loop. Walnut paneling. Looking out over Lake Michigan. In the distance to the East, you could see Gary, since the steel mills were no longer engulfing everything in smoke. The Governor congratulated me on finishing the marathon. When he learned I was in Military Intelligence, he said, 'Then you understand the past!' It was as if I knew some deep dark secret about money, or men, or something sinister, known by only a few. Continuing to relish the thrill of my race completion, I forced myself to look at this bigwig in his fancy office… quizzically."

"What was the secret?"

"Central banks—their ethics, I think. For the Governor said, 'Your father's going off to Basel to become part of the BIS. You know about the morals of money, don't you?' I felt I had to nod so as not to embarrass Lance, but I hadn't known."

"What did Lance say?"

"Nothing right then, but after we left he said, 'Remember the past. When you find its secrets, don't forget them.'" Jack paused. "You know, Sara, I'd really like to get into Lance's mind. As his son, I've failed in that regard. Doesn't every son or daughter want to know what their parents think?"

"Not that I've seen. My friends just think their parents are totally out of it. My friends are only interested in what's going on right now.

47

The kids I know are in their own world. Not in their parents' nostalgic yesteryear."

Watching her brother for his reaction, Sara saw that he had grown even more serious as he said, "To me, our father seems adrift. Maybe he takes comfort in the past. He's always comparing it to the present, as if the past was an instruction manual for today."

"Someday you can cross-examine our father."

"Or you will, Sara."

As brother and sister sat in the car in the driveway, Sara thought about querying her father, but soon their taxi arrived and they climbed in. Sara was going to the bus station and Jack to the airport. As they were leaving, Sara gestured toward the stucco Tudor house next door to their family's home. "Jack, remember the neighbors who lived there when we were young? I remember the mother, who was quite elderly, kept talking about the war and her son. It was obvious that she idolized her son and cherished her memories of him."

Jack nodded. "The Richards family. Yes, I remember. Bob was his name. He was an Army Captain—a pilot in World War II. Lost somewhere, I recall his mother saying. Many pilots were—crashed or shot down. I don't know what happened to him. Poor guy."

Then Jack was off to fly away once more. To a war somewhere. Afghanistan. And she was returning for her senior year in college. They had left their childhood home and their mother behind in a duet of hugs and brief goodbyes.

Sara had wanted to tell Jack about the time she was in the neighbor's home and had a strange experience, but for some reason she had held her tongue.

She and the elderly neighbor were looking at a photo album. When the mother got up to get her a snack, Sara had turned the page of the album and saw a picture of the son when he was little. About her age, he was looking straight at the camera. She had the distinct impression that he was looking at her, trying to tell her something. A chill crawled up her spine. As the mother came back with cookies, Sara had turned the page back. But when the neighbor turned the page again, to look at more photos, that picture of the little boy was nowhere to be seen.

The experience had given her an eerie omen that she couldn't quell.

*　　　*　　　*

Now, a year later, she was sitting in Kinkaid's office. Tears came to Sara's eyes, for that day at the lake, the cool Fall rain coming down on them, their drive through the bucolic Indiana countryside, being once again outside their home—those were her last memories of being with Jack. Oh, she pined, the sadness of certain memories. Yet others were joyful, while some... well... they were simply pop-up memories. Where were all these retro scenes housed in the human brain? Filed away as if in a cluttered cabinet? Or stored, like, in a deep mental freeze, to be thawed and served when you're mentally hungry? In what form and in what location, Sara mused, would her future memories be created? Would she relish them? As she was doing here—remembering her brother by being in her history professor's unconventional office.

CHAPTER ELEVEN:
THE COMMITMENT

Sara felt a bit uneasy in Kinkaid's office with him and Dr. Wolfe. She tried not to look at his absurd anti-aircraft desk. Maybe a conversation with these two would help her advance her career—turn into an invitation if offered to her to attend her private tomorrow. The think tank woman seemed determined to link her to Kinkaid's project. "The reason I'm here," Sara reminded herself, "is in response to Kinkaid's emotional and personal plea to me." Yes, she thought, I may be his last shot. Indeed, she reminded herself, 20th century history is her field and Kinkaid's.

She tried to answer Dr. Wolfe's question politely. "My parents... do you really want to know?"

"Yes, or I would not have asked."

"Well, my mother lives in Indianapolis in a modest house." Sara stopped. She wanted to get beyond this conversation and explore her motivation for being here. Telling about her parents was like going back into an earlier semester of life, one from which she had graduated. Sara hesitated, feigning a lack of interest, or was it a touch of boredom? "And my father in Switzerland."

"—As we've said, he is our banker in Basel." Dr. Wolfe was talking as if his employment and job location were of importance to their discussion.

Surprised, Sara hesitated before asking, "How did he become that?"

Kinkaid clarified, "Dr. Wolfe meant that your father is employed by the Bank for International Settlements."

Sara recalled that, in filling out her college application, she must have listed her parents' addresses along with her father's employment. Ditto on her student loan applications and her annual requests for scholarships. She guessed Kinkaid, and maybe everybody on the faculty and staff had access to her personal data. So much for student privacy.

As her attention followed the glass of wine handed to her by Dr. Wolfe, Sara noticed the rings and bracelets decorating the older woman's hands. Sara wished she could wear fashionable jewelry like that. Maybe some day. But first a job, a career... and possibly a husband. She wished her boyfriend were here with her. She was familiar with playing the boy-girl relationship scenario, as contrasted with her uncomfortable feeling as a member of this evening's troika.

After they raised their glasses in a toast, she took a sip. The cool liquid crept down her throat like a warning signal, or was it a wakeup call? Like the one you got when a final exam was coming up and you suddenly realized you weren't prepared. That was wakeup and panic combined. But now she felt no panic, only a growing momentum toward her future, and yes, along with it a wakeup call igniting her curiosity.

"Sara," Kinkaid began as if he were calling the class—her—to order for one of his lectures. "You have an opportunity to benefit from an important and long overdue undertaking. Let me label this meritorious pursuit more precisely: It is one of the world's most important and much needed historical research projects."

"I'm certainly flattered." Well, it is his pet project, Sara reflected.

Dr. Wolfe interrupted her thoughts, asking, "Have you ever been to Switzerland?"

"No," she replied simply.

"Would you like to go?" Dr. Wolfe answered, "Of course, you would."

"I couldn't possibly afford it," Sara said.

"Not a problem," came the assurance from Dr. Wolfe. "My foundation—"

"—Erika, let me explain."

Again, Sara sensed it was time for Kinkaid to fire the starting gun—like in one of Jack's marathons—trumpeting its "Go forward" to those behind the starting line who were braced to begin. But, she wondered, if this particular "Go" reflected instead a fear hanging over Kinkaid that, once sounded, no one would kick start from the blocks. In actuality, no one really was lined up or even watching from the sidelines. No one would hear the starting pistol. Except her. Right here. Now.

Kinkaid's voice fell to a whisper. "Sara, we are so sorry for the loss of your brother in Iraq, or was it Afghanistan?"

Sara smiled in reaction to his thoughtfulness. "There is a difference between them," she said in a slightly sarcastic tone, and wished she had not said it that way. In a softer voice, she added, "To me, it makes no difference the name of the country where he died— or its history, or its... What matters to me is that my brother Jack is no longer with us. What gain does his loss give to society? His death is a jewel stolen from me, and my mother, and my father." Except, she said to herself and then out loud, "I don't really know what my father thinks about Jack... or even about me."

"I wonder if he views life and people through ice-colored glasses, like most bankers," Dr. Wolfe said warmly.

"It must have been a terrible blow for him to have lost his only son," said Kinkaid.

My father is pretty cold. Like the dead, Sara thought. Cold, like my brother now.

*   *   *

Suddenly Sara conceived the idea of writing a letter to Jack, addressed to him wherever he was, or wherever his soul resided. In her mind she began to compose:

My Dear Brother Jack,

You may not be able to read this letter. Or perhaps in soldier heaven, which must be a different, more heroic and better place than normal heaven, you may be able to do so. Cherishing that hope and maybe belief, here goes:

In addition to Clio, the muse of history, there must be a muse of war. No, there cannot be because Zeus had nine daughters, each of whom became one of the muses. No daughter of an almighty deity as wise and powerful as Zeus would ever become the goddess of war. What daughter, what mother, what spouse, what woman wants war? I do not, and never did. But you did. You, Jack, obviously a healthy American male, intelligent and educated. What led you to war? What leader, what muse, what god, if there is one somewhere, ruling inside the Beltway in Washington, or topping the War Memorial Monument on the Circle in the center of downtown Indianapolis, or posing as the fountainhead atop our father's bank in Basel, Switzerland, led you to want to fight a war? Gods are not always male. Why did you not find a female goddess of peace on one of your marathon runs, with her running alongside you, advising? Would you not have listened to her? And be here today. With me.

Instead, Jack, you were paid money to fight, and in a currency honored 'round the world. And paid a healthy amount of this currency, plus medical and educational benefits—had you survived— medical care for life, special terms for a home loan, pension payments, burial rights in a VA cemetery (providing space is available). And now you have collected those last rights—those burial rights with a battery of gun salutes from a cadre of dress-uniformed military who, at the end of the memorial service, offered our mother a precision-folded American flag. Taps was bugled. We all stood motionless, rigid, at attention. Except, wantonly the tears flowed. You were laid to rest, not in a VA cemetery, but in our family plot in Crown Hill National Cemetery in Indianapolis. Congratulations! You got the last space on the hill near our beloved Hoosier poet, James Whitcomb Riley.

"Was all the money plus the tribute paid to you really worth it, Jack? Your life in exchange for that?" Sara realized she had uttered her last words out loud. She had been off in a personal area, in a very private zone. Lost. Ignoring her professor and the think tank matron.

Hearing her, Kinkaid said, "Sara, that is what I want you to find out." He hesitated and a tear forming—she could see—looked to Erika and said, "You answer her... please."

Somber, Erika said, "Gold." She tilted her glass and finished her drink. Then she poured more wine. "Gold," she repeated, drawing out the word as if the precious mineral was being tediously accumulated in a crude wooden sluice box at Sutter's Fort in the Gold Rush year of 1849. Or today extracted from mines around the world by low-paid, slave-like workers toiling deep in the Earth in hazardous conditions.

"You do know about money?" Kinkaid asked.

"Of course I do," Sara said.

"I mean gold—during the period of time you will be researching—gold was the standard for what people knew as value. Gold was the coin of each and every realm."

"But, Sir, it's hard to know much about something I haven't got," Sara stated simply.

Erika said, "You know about the ATM in the Student Union?"

54

"Which is closing—both it and the ATM."

"Your parents?" Erika asked.

"Just enough—obviously not gold—to get through this college"—Sara gestured around at the soon-closing campus—"and on to graduate school."

"Yes, Sara, we are offering you an opportunity that may well provide material for your doctorial dissertation." Dr. Wolfe smiled.

Kinkaid said, "To research the financial motivation for wars."

Erika added with firmness, "A unique career springboard."

Recovering his professorial composure, Kinkaid repeated the word, "Gold," adding, "Or rather, the abstraction. Or rather, the precious mineral. Or rather, the measure of monetary value." His words came at Sara in what she heard as a confusing array. She asked, "But which is the correct definition?"

"Each," he said.

"It's not a simple subject, then? Not just your basic gold bar?" She pointed to the bullion displayed in the Plexiglas case atop his Bofors desk."

Erika said, "The story of gold is as tarnished as the story of war."

Kinkaid said, "Centuries ago, the Spanish invaded and looted Central and South America for its gold and silver, shipping tons back to the rulers in Spain."

Sara asked, "Was that what became the Gold Standard?"

Take the Olympics for example: gold is awarded for first place; in banking, too, gold ranks above all metals. And worse, gold asserts its influence at the apex of human worth. Look around various places of worship. What do you see? Gold crosses, gold candlesticks, gold décor, like the old Spanish church in Quito, Ecuador and its entirely gilded interior."

Sara mused. "And banking?"

Erika said, "Banking's gold financed the war. That's what we want you to study, for we believe gold—much of it stolen by the Nazis— paid for the raw materials, the ammunition, the supplies to keep their soldiers fighting, their armies advancing as they looted even more gold treasures needed to provide food for the populations of Axis belligerents."

Kinkaid said, "Sara, your father can explain that each country's central bankers were charged with monitoring their country's gold, and they did it in Rougemont through The Bank for

International Settlements."

"The BIS, my father's bank, the world's central bank?" Sara said softly to herself. They nodded in assent.

Sara asked, "Can you please tell me how bankers, especially ones like my father, think? What are their values?"

"I could never be one of them. My way of thinking is not theirs," Kinkaid said. "That's one of the goals of our project—to find out how bankers, especially central bankers, think. And to learn their values and why they hold them."

Dr. Wolfe said. "Bankers' values are different from your and most professors populating the halls of academia. Or from those of us in non-profits or think tanks. It's true whether we're talking today about both genders, or in the time of World War II when bankers were exclusively male."

"In your research, Sara, you will encounter names like Henry Morgenthau, the American Secretary of the Treasury, Thomas McKittrick, head of the Bank for International Settlements in Switzerland during World War II, Montagu Norman, who ran the Bank of England, Carl Horace Greely Schatz, Adolf Hitler's war financier from Berlin, and later Emil Puhl, who ran the Reichsbank during the war, and Per Jacobsson, head of the Swedish Central Bank, and... oh yes, Yoneji Yamamoto of the Nippon Specie Bank, who spent most of the war in Berlin and in Switzerland, nearby in Bern."

"The American Horace Greely was a Nazi?"

Kinkaid explained, "No, Schatz's German parents lived in America for a time. They became so enamored with the story of Horace Greely that they gave their son Carl his middle name— making it a real mouthful."

Erika said, "Sara, these are some of the central bankers who financed the Nazi war machine. And they did so while living with their wives and children, socializing in an ancient chateau in the Swiss Alps." Dr. Wolfe put her arm around Sara and said, "With your research and writing, people will learn the real story behind that war and all wars."

With conviction, Kinkaid said, "Yes, Sara, my history project, long gathering dust, is now yours if you want it. I'm confident that with your hard work, people will learn the real story about World War II and all wars. "

"We want you to tackle this on your terms," Dr. Wolfe said. "You may not always agree with me, or us—for example, my statement about male dominance in banking. Matters such as these are yours to call during your investigation. My institute will publish your work. But you are independent. That way your findings will get the respect they deserve."

Kinkaid said, "We'd like you to begin right away." He put his arm around Dr. Wolfe's waist and squeezed in an affectionate embrace. "You tell her, Erika—woman to woman."

Dr. Wolfe's demeanor shifted from cordial to commanding, her voice changing from friendly to firm. "Your father is a small and facilitating cog in today's international banking world. He can help us learn a lot. If he is willing to."

"Will I be doing research on my father?"

"You will, but that's not all, by any means."

"I'll be seeing my father?"

"Yes. It's arranged. In Basel."

"For when?"

"If you accept our offer, you will fly to Geneva. I'll give you more details there at the Institute. Then you'll travel on to Basel where your father works. Afterward, you'll take a train up into the Alps." Dr. Wolfe looked intently at Sara. "We're offering you an opportunity that will allow you to begin your career as a historian researching the bankrolling of the Nazis in World War II. It's the real story behind all the wars in which so many have died, while so many industrialists have grown rich."

Reaching into his desk, Kinkaid produced two airline tickets and thrust them toward Sara's outstretched hand. She found herself automatically accepting them. Next came an envelope. "Here are Swiss francs, along with your personal bank card with a special chip. It accesses the Institute to End War's secret bank account in Zurich." He smiled at his new colleague. "You can use it at any ATM."

"And, of course, I'll have my computer with me for Internet access."

"Of course."

"This is all a bit overwhelming. Still, yes, I'd like to do this. It will be an incredible adventure. I'll have to tell my mother. And my father, of course. "

"I'm delighted," said Kinkaid. "You were my most promising

student, Sara. I think you'll find this a rich vein to explore, if you'll excuse the pun."

"Your flight is two weeks away," said Dr. Wolfe. "I trust that will give you enough time to wrap things up here?"

"Dr. Wolfe, if I have any questions about what I'll need to bring with me, can I call you?"

"Of course. Here's my card. It has all my contact information. And, of course, I'll see you in Geneva."

Sara graciously accepted the card and then hugged Dr. Wolfe. "Thank you for your faith in me. Well, I better be off. I've got to get busy on my PhD program."

CHAPTER TWELVE:
SARA IN GENEVA

Two weeks later, following meetings with her professors in the History department at the big state university and especially with her PhD advisor, each to whom Professor Kinkaid had arranged introductions, Sara eagerly boarded a plane and departed for Switzerland. If nothing else, she thought in her excitement, this was going to be an amazing way to see Switzerland and the Alps.

Having negotiated passport control at the Geneva International Airport, Sara followed the signs directing her to the taxi queue. The long flight had been her first adventure in the air, and now this European country was her initial excursion outside Indiana. Oh, maybe Kentucky for the Derby, or Illinois, and once to Ohio for a college debating contest. People in those places had seemed to her a tad strange from those she knew in her more familiar environs, but not alarmingly so. How different were these people in Switzerland going to be? On her walk to the taxis, Sara instructed herself to stay alert, to observe, and take it all in with an open mind.

Climbing into the first available taxi, Sara named her destination. The driver nodded and drove directly to the office building housing the Institute to End War. It was a drab gray granite International Style building on a hillside where it was dwarfed by the gloomy failure of the nearby and similarly designed 1920's League of Nations complex. Looking at the larger array, Sara recalled reading how the League had been the hope of the world to bring lasting peace after The Great War. What became World War I had been "the war to end all wars," as Woodrow Wilson had proclaimed it once America entered the conflict and was deep in fighting it. From her readings, Sara concluded Wilson had hoped to make the war, and the resultant peace when it did come, a cause for people to rally around. But after the 1918 Armistice, he had failed to entice the isolationists in the American Congress to allow the United States to join the League.

They didn't want to endorse a worldwide endeavor to ensure world peace. Instead, they viewed the League as limiting America's freedom by threatening its autonomy.

Outside, as the Swiss sun began to set, Sara watched the Institute's building darken as it lost the battle to compete with the shadow cast by the massive headquarters of the League of Nations. The old International Style of architecture seemed to her to lose its majesty as the brief invading dusk gave way to the nighttime darkness that now cloaked the streetscapes of Geneva.

This was Geneva, one of the great cities of ever-neutral Switzerland. The League of Nations promise had faded quickly. Sara recalled that both Japan and Germany withdrew from membership, and then the Italians invaded Ethiopia. The abiding hope that another world war could be avoided had dimmed. Yes, the memory of The Great War had also died away. The world forgot its killings of millions of troops who perished in the trench warfare, the millions of tons of shells fired, the horrors of poison gas attacks. In her History of Psychiatry course at JWR, Sara had learned about the psychological toll the war had taken on those soldiers who were lucky enough to make it back home, only to face mediocre medical help.

In the Institute's large reception area, Sara was overwhelmed by the seemingly never-ending murals adorning the walls. Punctuated with grim gravestones, each frame showed a war, some war, some she'd never heard of, others of course known to her. The overwhelming presence of war—everywhere in the room—caused her to choke up. As she became immersed in each of the panels, with each scene, each war, each battle, each death, the image of Jack filled Sara's mind.

In the background of each mural, the artist had painted scenes of industrial complexes turning out war materials: trucks, tanks, airplanes, rockets, bullets, and artillery shells, along with weapons unknown to her. Smokestacks billowed with the smoke of profits for factory owners. Subtly painted into the backdrop of some scenes were images of the factory owners—identified by their tuxedos and evening gowns—stacking their profits into towering piles of chips on green felted tables. They were drinking martinis and smiling broadly as if they owned the wars and were reaping the financial benefits therefrom.

Where in these paintings, Sara asked herself, was depicted the ideology of peace? Clearly not in the winnings stacked in the front of the rich and satisfied industrialists. The scenes overshadowed the battlefield below where soldiers lay dead or wounded.

"How awful for those fighting," Sara said out loud, then to herself, yet how profitable for those who owned the weapon machines, at least according to the muralist's art. Sara's gaze wandered one more time across the paintings, each signed in the bottom right corner by the artist. She looked closer at the signature: "BarbaraK" in each panel—the muralist, and her underlying inspiration, as it must have developed in painting the scenes. Was the artist commissioned by Erika Wolfe? Of course, she presumed. In the same manner Sara was to be supported for her research and writing. The Institute's promises for sponsorship of the muralist had surely been kept. She assumed hers would be also.

Returning to the message of the murals, Sara thought about the many wars illustrated. Wars were seemingly continuous. One led to another, so it appeared from the murals. Where was peace? There was no mural portraying peace. Peace was implied, perhaps subliminally suggested as an interlude, a recess, now and again, lasting for a time too brief to warrant its own mural.

Questions as to the reasons for each of these wars filled her mind. Were they fought to acquire territory? Not territory for the men fighting, but instead for the rulers who had persuaded the men to fight. Were wars a revolt against oppression? Did they alleviate monetary oppression? For the men fighting? Or only for their leaders, enabling them to grow richer? Were some wars begun to combat leaders' jealousies of other leaders? Thinking of the many Christian Crusades, Sara said to herself: for sure, some wars had been promulgated by religious zealots—pitting one set of spiritual beliefs against another, splitting hairs of dogma and creating divine motivation that would persuade men to fight and die, each for their own god of motivation. An image of such a deity failed to appear in her mind.

Yet all of these conflicts presumably had been fostered and fought by intelligent men—yes, and some women—but why would intelligent people want to kill other people? From her classes in psychology, Sara recalled her professor categorizing the styles of thinking that, given their own unique mindset, men and women were likely to follow. Attorneys thought one way, engineers another, artists still a different way, and so forth, styles following vocations. But war was not a vocation. What went through someone's mind leading to initiate a war? To fight the wars, there was the need and the pressure and the technical advances by war profiteers to engineer and manufacture bigger and better weapons with accompanying bigger and better profits. Those motivations paralleled campaigns to recruit even more men to die, urged onward by the hype generated by a leader's promoted cause, be it Capitalism, Communism, Socialism, anarchy, religion…

Brother Jack, brave and strong, fit and intelligent, no slouch in resisting propaganda's persuasion, had allowed himself to become a pawn in one of these wars. Was his war depicted among the murals? Did his war have a name? To be chiseled into his tombstone? There, for all time! The War in Afghanistan.

So engrossed was she in wars that when Dr. Wolfe appeared, Sara didn't return the older woman's offered handshake or respond politely to her welcoming smile. Until, "Ms. Vogel, I'm glad you could meet me this late in the day. I see you have become absorbed in our murals."

Sara nodded and asked, "Who is the muralist, BK?"

"Barbara Kaleesh. She's a Middle Eastern refugee. Educated in art school in Italy before she returned to the chaos of war in her home country. She's anti-war, as are we at IEW. You could say we discovered her."

Sara sensed an affinity with Barbara Kaleesh. She smiled at Erika and said, "But why me, Dr. Wolfe?"

"Call it luck if you want, but luck only applies when there's talent behind it."

Sara said softly, "Thank you."

Erika motioned for Sara to follow. "Please come into my office." Visualizing Jack by her side, walking tall and strong with her to address her new assignment, Sara followed in silence. A few steps on, Dr. Wolfe attempted pleasantries about her flight. Sara failed to respond. Instead, entering Wolfe's office, she blurted, "Erika, where am I to begin my research? And what am I looking for? I mean, for what am I looking?"

After pouring two glasses of Swiss Neuchatel wine, the host motioned for Sara to sit beside her on a red leather couch. Erika waited for the duo of sips ritual, in the process toasting "peace," before slowly replying, "In the secret chateau…"

Sara said, "Secret?"

Erika nodded. "It's no secret the chateau is there. The secret is that no one knows much about the story that unfolded among the people who lived the war years there—certainly not the conversations that took place during their games of bridge and strolls along Alpine trails looking for wildflowers." Erika turned on her computer. "Watch this earlier YouTube video from the UK about financing Hitler. There's a brief mention of Rougemont. You'll get the gist."

After watching, Sara said, "Well, then, if no one knows more about those years, how am I to conduct my research?" She added, "And how do we know who was inside the chateau?" Sara's tone of voice, perhaps caused by her frustration, by the message of the murals, by Jack not being by her side to calm her with his big brother demeanor troubled her. She lamented, "The video doesn't tell us much."

"You said you are seeking a challenge."

"I am. I'm just hoping you can point me in the right direction," Sara said, asking, "Do you know any local historians I can consult? Or is there a town hangout I should know about? Where can I meet some old timers? Perhaps a bartender who will tell stories about World War II?"

"Not likely, given the decades that have passed—three-quarters of a century. No, there are no centenarians around—not even in the local pubs—who might obligingly recite oral history. Even if there were, it is unlikely back then they would have been admitted inside the chateau. But I don't want to dissuade you completely. You should certainly ask around."

Sara said, "You're basically suggesting the walls of this secret chateau will speak to me, albeit cryptically, while I record their French or German words in the app on my cell phone. Or will the chateau speak in down home Hoosier English?" Her angst growing, Sara finished off her wine.

Erika refreshed their glasses.

Sara sat uncomfortably in the leather sofa, scolding herself for her irritable remark. She said, "I'm sorry. I'm just befuddled."

Erika smiled.

Sara said, "How do you know about this old chateau? And why is it so secret?"

"Fair questions."

Sara waited.

Erika said, "There were real people inside this out-of-the-way place in this out-of-the way village—men who were financing the war around them in Europe and Africa and Asia... and throughout the world."

"Were there any women?"

"Yes, of course. And children." Erika hesitated, then added, "Servants, too. From Skip's earlier investigation, he and I know the names of the people, the BIS central bankers and the names of some of their wives and children." Erika added, "They were from countries that were at war with each other. Certain neutral countries also had representatives."

"Do we know the names of the servants?"

"No. I'm hoping you will find out. Back then servants were considered to be lesser people. At Rougemont, for us, they may prove to be important. There were seven."

Sara felt no need to conceal her state of mind. "Where do I begin?"

Erika raised her glass in a new toast and said, "Now, we are approaching the starting line."

Sara envisioned one of Jack's starting lines at a race. She saw her brother in his sleek running shorts emblazoned with the Indiana state flag with its 19 stars—one for each state admitted to the Union prior to 1839. Together with other male and female athletes, Jack was lined up behind a line drawn across some boulevard, each participant poised to start, mentally gearing up, calling upon their physical and mental resources to guide them in the undertaking of a super-human task—running more than 26 miles; no, racing the full marathon distance, pushing their personal limits, and achieving the virtually impossible goal of victory, or of at least a respectable time. Sara felt she, too, was about to start off pursuing a similarly challenging goal. She wondered if she could bring her endeavor to a respectable conclusion.

CHAPTER THIRTEEN:
TO LOOK FOR

Dr. Wolfe lowered her voice, suggesting to Sara that she was about to share a secret. "We've learned that there is a document that may be a servant's diary, or perhaps it's a series of writings, like a memoir. None of us has seen it."

"How do you know about this document?"

"Skip and I learned that the chateau was recently sold. The public record of the sale shows an inventory of the seller's antiques— required public information for sales of historical landmarks. The document states that the sellers were to remove every item listed. However, appended to the list and dated days later and likely overlooked by the sellers when they hauled their antiques away, and possibly unknown to them, or of no perceived value to them, are documents with labels ranging from old photo albums of the chateau to 'A series of writings from World War II'."

Sara whistled. "A memoir from one of the servants who worked there?"

"We hope so."

"Where is it now?"

"We don't know. Hopefully lying around in the chateau somewhere, possibly in the servant's quarters."

Sara asked, "Who was the seller of the chateau?"

Erika said, "Here's what we do know: The BIS bankers came to Rougemont in 1941. At that time the U.S. was still neutral. An American lawyer, Thomas McKittrick, was voted by the other central bankers to head up the bank. An aristocratic American friend, William Hallam Tuck from Maryland, owned Chateau Rougemont. Tuck made it available to his friend and the BIS as a wartime refuge."

"Why didn't the BIS continue to meet in Basel?"

"Basel was close to the war zone and vulnerable to Nazi invasion. The Germans remained a threat to Switzerland's neutrality. In the event of a German invasion, the Swiss planned to abandon their lowlands and retreat to defend their mountain communities. Rougemont is up in the Alps, close to the Swiss capital at Bern where the embassies, including the American and German, continued to function. The city's diplomatic section was full of spies and rumors and intrigue."

Sara imagined dark streets with men lurking in doorways, like Orson Wells as Harry Lime in "The Third Man Theme." She imagined the moon shining on men in trench coats, men who were conspiring, selling secrets, perhaps being murdered, or if more fortunate, pocketing payoffs for information about the movement of armies and the movement of money. All this was taking place in Bern and in the village of Rougemont. "So, Erika, do you know who is the new owner of the chateau? Or maybe it is a secret owner?"

"Alas, we don't know."

"But where am I to look. If there's a new owner, how do you think I can get inside to explore?" Sara paused and asked if the vintage antiques had indeed been removed. "Maybe this memoir was locked away in the drawer of one of the antique pieces and taken away."

Erika said, "We believe all the antiques are gone. Two people in the village, to whom I spoke last week, told me that they saw moving vans loading up what they said was everything. That was days before the sale was set to close. Skip and I think that because the World War II memoir was listed separately from the long list of antiques, in their haste, the sellers may not have known about it. The new caretaker may know. You'll recall that Skip—that is your professor—mentioned his nemesis, a Dr. Ellis."

Sara nodded.

"Skip recommended him for the job through the real estate agent handling the transaction."

"But we don't know who the new owner is. The agent wouldn't tell us, and the deed on file in the canton records is in an untraceable name."

"And the BIS—their archives?" Sara asked.

"Frankly, the BIS would like it better if this chapter in their history remains unwritten," Dr. Wolfe said. "But you might have better luck."

"What do we hope is in this diary, or memoir?"

"It's primary source material and may have all sorts of details about the world's central bankers. In those days servants were not supposed to listen to conversations, but in reality they heard everything. We don't know whether they understood what they overheard. But they could describe what was taking place. We want to know how these central bankers paid for World War II, how their minds worked, and why the war was allowed to begin and continue for so many years."

"Wouldn't such a memoir be an incredible source of information!" Sara proclaimed. "But what if I find it and discover it's only about mundane things, not about the BIS bankers and their wives?"

"You never know. Eyewitness accounts usually contain extremely valuable information. I'm terribly optimistic." Erika handed her an envelope and said, "Here's your hotel reservation for tonight and your plane ticket. I've a taxi waiting outside. Tomorrow you'll fly to Basel."

Sara nodded. "But—"

"—Here are some relevant notes for you to review tonight." Erika handed Sara a manila envelope. "Along with more suggestions on how you might pursue your search." She gestured to a sheet, "Here is the URL for our special IEW Internet research site, a search engine designed especially for professionals such as yourself. You do have your computer with you?"

Sara patted her pack.

"Oh, I almost forgot. Do look up Elsa… the local librarian. I talked to her once on the phone. Quite knowledgeable about local matters. But she's active in some sort of neo-Nazi political party, so be prepared for her to rant about the merits of fascism."

*   *   *

Sara saw the taxi, its light turned off, indicating it was engaged. The driver proved courteous, opening the door for her.

"Sara, my name's Pierre," he announced. Entering the traffic flow, he announced, "Hotel Higgs Boson."

Sara smiled. "How did you know my name?"

"I know a lot," he said. "I have a useful contact for you in Rougemont."

"Really?" Sara was beginning to feel she'd become part of a spy novel.

"Yes, a woman—Lena. She runs the Tourist Office. Ask about her mother."

"Her mother?" Sara's mind briefly went to her own mother, but she was impatient to get to the hotel, shower, have something to eat, and then look over the information Dr. Wolfe had given her. She hoped she could put the murals on the walls of the Institute out of her mind, but doubted she'd be able to.

Pierre said, "Her mother was German."

Sara digested that bit of information as the taxi pulled up in front of the hotel.

"The fare's on the Institute to End War," Pierre said. "Tip, too. Remember, when you get to the little town of Rougemont, ask for Lena. Tell her I sent you."

Sara thanked Pierre, who told her he would collect her in the morning for the trip to the airport. Inside the hotel, the receptionist was polite, overly so, Sara thought, giving her a room key and telling her in detail about the menu for tomorrow's breakfast, the times and where in the hotel it would be served.

Over dinner, which she had served in her hotel room, Sara opened the packet from Dr. Wolfe. Too much data, too much to think about. Sara felt overwhelmed. Everything began to swarm in on her, melding her fatigue into the assignment, the murals, travel, jet lag. She tumbled into sleep moments after she laid her head on the bed pillow, fully intending to read through Erika's notes, which began with a list of the children who had joined their parents to live in the chateau during the war years. Even a baby. Quite new, quite little.

*   *   *

Sara was back on campus. It was deserted, abandoned, lonely, quiet, and she was by herself, searching for Manny, for Kyra, for her friends. She wanted to show them her baby, which she cuddled warmly in her breasts. She stopped to nurse, to love, to cherish. She sat on a bench by the student union building, now shuttered. Out of the blue, Manny strutted past, smiling a look of male possessiveness and was promptly gone, out of her sight. Was he the baby's father? He said something about marriage. Casual like, for he wasn't one to be formal. In her dream, Sara screamed, waking herself up. Lying atop the bedspread, still fully clothed, she exclaimed to the hotel room, "Wait a minute! I didn't have sex! Well... Maybe... No, we did not!" She saw Manny's body, fully revealed in its male configuration. In confusion, she spoke again to the room, "Sex... maybe... but I don't have a baby. For God's sake, I'm not pregnant! Nor have I been. Nor do I want to be, at least not now. But my body is telling me it craves a baby." She said, "Body! Behave! I've a career to pursue. My assignment is my priority. That's what I'm here to address."

CHAPTER FOURTEEN:
BASEL, THE BANK FOR INTERNATIONAL
SETTLEMENTS, AND SARA'S FATHER

Sara couldn't conceal, yes, her delight, or was it? His slight half-wave, obvious to her as she exited the turbo-prop commuter aircraft from Geneva, was at best perfunctory. Her father. It had been how many years from their last ever-so-brief conversation? She had no trouble recognizing him. How did he know which flight she would be on? Oh, yes, Dr. Wolfe had told her it had been arranged. Before negotiating the portable stairway down from the plane, she looked intently at the older man. He was in a blue blazer with creased tan trousers, a stylish fedora, shiny pointed shoes— Italian, she guessed—a small red carnation in his lapel. Dapper? Well... maybe for an older man. Yes, for her father. She felt a sense of pride for her father, who was clutching an attaché case—likely leather—in his left hand. He looked laundered, proper, financially fixed, an integral player in the money and culture of Switzerland. And, she asked herself, of the financial world? Yes, it was her father. She tabulated the years—four, or maybe by now a little more. He tipped his hat, and she gave him her own slight wave in return. How should she verbally greet this distant banker father? Having been away from her for so long a time, both geographically and emotionally. What would he say? What would she say?

The Basel airport was in France, west across the Rhine from Switzerland. On the skyline to the east, Sara could see the multi-storied blue-tinged tower of the Bank for International Settlements rising, blending into the azure Swiss sky, right where Dr. Wolfe said it would be—a modern circular spire adding its note to the crenellated Alps on the horizon beyond. The building would house, Sara surmised, the office from which her father had this morning traveled. Or maybe, instead, he had come from his home, or apartment, or wherever he lived. Maybe with a woman? Why not his wife, her mother, here with him? That question remained unanswered with only a hint of a clue—the thought of parents getting on in years and being estranged clouded her thoughts.

There he was. Her father. She, his daughter. Two Hoosiers, long apart, years apart, now meeting in a foreign land. About to embrace? So she hoped. That was her question as she descended toward him, he remaining stationary. Soon his arms rose and stretched forward toward her—a marionette, as if controlled by some higher paternal command. Momentarily he was enveloping her in an embrace as she, in return, kissed his shaven cheek, her tears of joy flowing. Perhaps there were even tears from him. She couldn't tell, nor was it important. He was her father. She felt familial comfort for the first time in a long time—ever since that last day with Jack, and Jack was gone. Forever? Oh, yes, forever.

"Sara."

"Mr. Vogel," she managed. "Dad" or "Father" had never worked for her, for dads and fathers were always there for you, not off somewhere else... But then she remembered Jack's story and said, "Lance," sensing his smile and feeling him hugging her again, this time tighter.

Releasing her, Lance said, "Come, I'll show you Basel and my BIS." He appended, "With its past—the past into which you will be looking."

Yes, that was why she was here—the BIS, but not the BIS of today—the BIS back then, three-quarters of a century ago. She said as much. He grunted his understanding of that period of history, expressed in his non-verbal sound. "Yes," he added in a nostalgic tone, "the 1930s were the headiest of times." He let silence underline his statement and then added, "I've a car and driver."

*   *   *

She handed her pack to the uniformed driver and, following Lance, climbed into the backseat.

"The tower," Lance instructed. As they crossed the bridge over the Rhine into Basel, he told her, "In those war days, many French refugees—Jews and those fleeing the Nazis—crossed here seeking refuge from the spreading war. Seeking safety. Switzerland was safe then—at least for that moment, maybe only a brief moment. No one knew about the next day, or week, or month. Rumors flew, suggesting a multitude of possibilities—the Nazis would invade Switzerland tomorrow; the French would surrender to Hitler any minute; the British might bomb Basel; everyone might die in a Nazi blitzkrieg." His tone was dire, yet almost philosophical, she thought. "But you knew all that before you came here, didn't you?"

Sara nodded. As she looked at the bridge and then the river flowing below, Sara imagined the refugees, forlorn, hungry, carrying babies perhaps, pushing buggies with children, all of them hoping against hope for freedom, for safety for themselves and especially their children as they approached the Swiss border guards, all the while looking over their shoulders for soldiers coming after them. German soldiers? French soldiers? Would they get across the border bridge and pass through the Swiss checkpoints? Or be turned back? To face what? "The refugees, oh my God!" she heard herself exclaim.

Lance said, "Knowing about it doesn't make it any easier to understand."

As they drove on, Sara said, "What an awful time in history." Then silence, she deep in thought.

The driver let them out in the BIS porte cochere. Lance guided her through the security checkpoint, the guard saluting and addressing him by name, yet carefully inspecting her pack. Then into an elevator. Midway up the tower, passing through four floors, Lance gestured and said, "These are my floors. For when the important people come to Basel."

"Who are they?"

"Central bankers from each of the major countries. For their two days of meetings, dinners, and parties. Every calendar quarter."

"You're in charge of—"

"—The arrangements: space for their meetings, elaborate gourmet dinners, wine… entertainment. Each central bank has a suite for its director with private space for its staff." He added as if it was of little import, yet important to tell her, "And there is a nuclear bomb shelter under the basement." By way of explanation, he said, "In a catastrophe, it is important to safeguard the people who run central banks." He looked intently at his daughter and declared, "You see, bankers and banking is most important for the entire world— for civilization."

Higher up, the elevator stopped and the door opened. Lance led her along a drab beige and brown colored hallway toward a corner office overlooking both the modern and the historic city of Basel. Rather than plunking himself down in the ergonomic chair behind his sleek polished wooden desk, Lance eased into position beside her on the inviting red leather sofa.

She noticed his desk was devoid of anything—papers, telephone—the exception being an Apple computer, keyboard, and track pad. A cell phone, small with a petite cord leading to a tiny earplug, peeked out at her from his blazer pocket. A small white placard framed in silver was mounted next to the computer. In small but bold black letters it read: "To my fellow Americans, BIS deposits are not insured by the FDIC; instead, we here at the BIS insure the FDIC."

Sara gestured toward the placard. "Is that true?"

Lance smiled. He apparently thought her question amusing, for he chuckled and said, "That's what I tell visiting Americans to emphasize the importance of the BIS."

Looking down on them from the dull beige wall behind his desk loomed a row of a dozen—Sara counted—black and white framed photographs of ever-so-serious looking men—none smiling—in outdated attire. Sara didn't ask about them, other than to presume that, at some time in the past, they had been the central bankers running the BIS.

For a moment she thought she detected a golden halo ringing each head. Then, if they had been there at all, the crowns of light vanished.

Instead of asking about the men or inquiring where were the women, she blurted, "Why did you meet me, Lance?" She worried her question was too abrupt. "I mean... Lance (it was feeling more comfortable) it's so good to see you. After such a long time. Mother sends her love."

Not addressing her question, Lance said simply, "Jack's gone," his tone having shifted from visitor explanatory to fatherly grief.

Sara nodded solemnly.

For the ensuing moments father and daughter sat together in silence. To Sara it was their attempt at a memorial to her brother, Lance's son. Thoughtfully, Lance soon broke the silence by saying, "Needless loss."

"He would disagree."

"But he's not here to do so, is he?"

"No," Sara began to cry. Lance seemed to shed a tear, then recovered, his mind seeming to drift off somewhere. She wondered where his thoughts had gone. To the past? To little Jack growing up? Except, as she recounted the few times her father had appeared in her life, he had seldom been present in family pictures, so how could he be harboring paternal memories? Even of her? She had few of him. Certainly none accurate or applicable for their meeting today.

"Jack and I spent a nice day up at the lake when he was home on leave."

"Before he went back to Afghanistan?"

Sara nodded.

"How was he?"

"Determined to go back, despite my pleading. He said it was his duty."

Her father didn't say anything in response. Breaking the silence, she asked, "What else do you do here? That is, between these quarterly meetings of the central bankers?"

"Didn't they explain at the Institute to End War?"

"Only what the BIS is and why it exists, but not what you do day after day." Maybe she didn't care to know. But why not?

"In our last conversation—"

"—You remember?"

"—Of course, Sara. That day I explained a bit of the history of the BIS to you."

"Yes, I recall you saying that back in 1930 its reason for being was to distribute German reparations from the Great War to the Allied countries."

"Good." Silence. Waiting.

Sara went on, "That entailed moving gold from the German Central Bank to other recipient central banks, so that each country would get its rightful share of the Versailles reparations."

His gaze turned penetrating, seeming to question the term "rightful." His voice rising, he remarked, "Gold."

Sara said, "Yes, gold bullion—bars."

"Correct."

Sara asked, "But then…"

"Looming Nazi expansion soon turned to aggression as the 1930s moved on—the appeasement at Munich, the Sudetenland—what very soon became the Second World War. But first, Sara, tell me what you learned about who made up the BIS back then?"

She gestured at the photographs on the wall and asked, "Where were the women?"

"Wives? There were no women bankers, at least not running the BIS."

"Wives, then?"

"You suppose correctly. They each had wives."

"Is that a good thing?" Sara wondered at what his answer might mean. Was his wife—the woman who was her mother—a good thing for him? And why? Or how? Other than gender obvious.

"They were couples."

"Two unequal people?"

"Unequal?" He seemed taken aback. "Certainly equal in the eyes of the law, for they were legally linked."

Sara didn't agree. "But not in practical matters." She recalled learning about the historic sea changes coming out of the women's movement, especially in the US. While she didn't want to argue with her father, she tried, "But were they—the couples, I mean—emotionally equal? With each other?"

"Yes, I suppose, certainly by their vows recited," Lance's tenor was as if he was reading a rulebook for gender behavior.

"As couples, they were together here in Basel in 1939?"

Lance nodded. "Yes, from 1930 on, they were right here in Basel. Even after the war began in '39. And continually during the long dark war years."

"All that time?"

Lance went to a drawer behind his desk and extracted a greenish wine bottle. "Neuchatel?"

Taken aback, Sara shook her head. Lance poured himself a goblet of the white wine, raised it toward his daughter, sipped, and reflected. "They drank together," he said.

"Who?"

"These central bankers as they determined whose national gold was whose."

"The gold was here?"

"Oh, no."

"Where?"

"In vaults in the various countries, some in England, some in the

U.S. Sometimes they didn't know for sure, given the Nazi occupation of so many European countries."

"But Switzerland was not invaded?"

Lance nodded. "But in fear the war would spill across the Rhine and into Switzerland, which was neutral, the entire BIS boarded steam trains and traveled up into the mountains on the new rail line to Chateau d/Ox. Moved the entire staff and records of the BIS into the Hotel du Parc."

"Wives, too?"

"Wives, children, babies if they had them. Plus servants, many of whom were local, and BIS staff members from different countries—chosen for their knowledge of money, gold, and experience with central banking."

Sara said, "But you haven't answered my question."

"Which one?"

"That was before. My question is: what do you do now or did you do when you came to the BIS when I was in grade school? After you left the bank in our home town, went to the Federal Reserve Bank in Chicago, and then here to Basel?"

"Actually, Sara, I'm not supposed to talk about it." Lance poured another glass. "It was secret. You see, a few years after the Berlin Wall came down, I was approached to apply to join a secret part of the U.S. Government."

Sara showed her surprise, maybe even disbelief. "The CIA? You, a spy?"

"Not exactly. Rather, they were looking for someone with extensive knowledge to research the world's gold supply—where it is stowed."

"Is that's how Jack got into Military Intelligence?"

"—Probably."

"But why didn't Mother come with you to Basel?"

"You two were in school. She wouldn't leave. Besides, your mother cannot keep a secret, and she's... well... She would have been deemed a security risk."

"Did you ever think abut divorcing my mother?"

Lance nodded. "Divorce in the CIA is a career killer. Makes the divorced partner a target for enemy agents. So, no, we simply parted ways."

"Do you have someone here?"

"What if I did? What would you think?"

"I don't know. I hadn't thought about it much."

They sat in silence, Sara's unspoken questions lingering on her lips.

Lance drank and talked once more. "Tomorrow you are going farther up the rail line to Rougemont." He gestured toward the wine bottle. She nodded. He produced a wine glass and poured. "There resides the key question: which country owned what amount of gold."

"After the Nazis took them over—"

"—One by one. Country after country." Lance lamented, "In rapid succession—across Europe." He sat in silence for a moment sipping his drink until the glass was empty.

Sara waited. Finally she said, "Before I left, and on the plane flying over—on my e-reader—I read books about the history of the war."

"The battles. The espionage. The displaced people. The camps. The killings…" Lance grew silent. Then he stood, went to the corner window and gazed out over Basel. "Sara, I said those were heady times."

Nodding to indicate that she was curious to hear more, she waited.

"Back then in the 1930s, everything was defined in its own established and agreed-upon place. It was as if the world had a printed program with names and numbers of everyone. Each person lived a prescribed role, whose duties everyone agreed upon. As uncertain as the world was, everything and everybody were in their assigned roles, defined by destiny and by common agreement. Prejudices and bigotry abounded, yes, but they were defined. Everyone knew them, respected the constant boundaries. You could rely on them."

Sara felt ill. Disbelief is not easy within any family where unity is treasured, she told herself. Disbelief in her father's words was upsetting her. How dare he hold such beliefs? Was he so warped as to subscribe to what he was saying? Surely not!

To her further consternation, Lance went on. "By the mid-1930s, the Nazi Aryans were strategically in charge of the Western world. The German people were happy, superior, the best of the human crop—in their minds the superior litter from Mother Earth. The Jews were either numb to their future or fleeing for their lives. It was as if everyone and every place were defined in a dictionary of world values. That was the beauty of those years. Still is. Even in hindsight. For me."

Sara shut her ears, but Lance went on. She couldn't seal off his words. "Not like it is today—a world in chaos: riots, demonstrations, migrations, refugees, uncertainties." He grew silent. It was as if, in Sara's judgment, her father was mentally reliving times past, somehow going back to a distant place—a historic, lost culture of old—an anthropologist in a vintage roadster joy riding down life's old byways with no GPS for guidance, no brakes, and no guardrails.

Hesitatingly, Sara asked, "You talk as if you had personally experienced these years and these feelings. But you didn't live back then, did you? So how do you have this firsthand knowledge of those long-ago times?"

"I was not yet born… not 'til after the war, and that's what hung up my CIA application. I couldn't produce my birth certificate. Still can't. You see, when I joined the BIS, they didn't require one."

Sara thought about that question and about her feelings as to his 1930's remarks. She asked, "Then how do you know the feelings of the people back then?"

Lance looked at her sternly, "I've followed the money. You see, Sara, along with society's money goes its emotions, its rules, its directions, and especially peoples' feelings, all of which make up history. That gives us stability, and everyone yearns for the safety of stability."

Yes, she guessed stability was good. But didn't stability suggest stagnation?

Lance looked intently at her. "You probably wonder why I left Indiana? And why I tell you these things now."

She waited.

"I have always been curious about the world, about its money."

Sara felt an urge to laugh, but didn't. She sat still, trying to be calm, waiting.

"There were no answers in Indianapolis, nor in Chicago, so I wrangled the job here in Basel. I'm still searching for answers."

"For which questions?" She added, "Like, why you left your wife, my mother, us—your family?"

"A mistake," he allowed. "I'm trying to make up for it now, here with you, don't you see?"

"No."

"There are answers in libraries and other archives."

"To what?"

Lance said slowly, "Sara, when you studied in your college library, what did you feel?"

"Pressure. Like I had to write a paper. Under a deadline. And then go with others to the student union to talk about our assignment."

"I mean, something else."

"What?"

"It's what I often experience in a library when I am surrounded by books. Looking at them, sometimes I can see all their words—well, not all the words—but all the authors' imagination behind his or her words. In each and every book. It's all there to see, to feel, to try to understand. I feel I can see back in time, or more accurately feel, see, experience the forces at work in those historic times."

Sara's thoughts drifted back to her classroom and Kinkaid's Bofors antiaircraft desk. She acknowledged, "That does sound kind of crazy, I will admit. In fact, Lance, you sound crazy." Right away she was embarrassed for being so direct. Yet she had to admit having similar experiences at times herself. But she was reticent to share that with her father.

For only a moment her father looked at her, showing, she worried, anger at her. Then his look softened, becoming reflective, as he said, "You know, Sara, I've never told anyone my observations about the 1930s." He paused, and then said more forcefully, "Forget what I said...forget it!"

Sara wondered if her father had bouts of hallucination, caused by sessions with marijuana or some other stimulant. She realized how little she really knew about her father. Absently she said, "Most history is written by men."

"Who else? There was no other gender to do it," Lance said. "Until the women's movement, gender roles were precisely defined and rigid."

She asked, "Like in the 1930s? So, tell me more about those days."

"Those days counted in the ticking clock of history."

"But did they count any more than days do today?"

"That's your task, Sara. That's why you are here. Isn't your motivation to find out how the past continues to shape the present?" For once, Lance smiled at his daughter.

Sara sensed she was in a play—on stage, with no script, groping for her lines, the right lines, while everyone else on the stage and out there in the audience was following and reading from their personal copy of the script. A contemplative Sara felt the surprise of the unknown. What had she gotten herself into? Well, she'd gotten a grant. Money. Seemingly a lot of money, too, at least a lot to her. Money on which to live, to travel, to buy new clothes. Enough Euros and Swiss francs to begin to pay back the principal and interest on her student loans. To begin research on her dissertation for her hopefully coming PhD degree. Now she could think, yes, maybe even plan for her future. Perhaps romance. Possibly a marriage? A baby? Sheesh, not now, she told herself. Yet for sure, the career of a lifetime. Maybe? Exciting. Was this not a golden opportunity for her to make a name for herself as a female historian? What if she could indeed do so? Wow!

Sara broke the silence of her ruminations. "But, Lance, why are you so interested in the past? Is that your job at the BIS—to chronicle, and even extol the past? Are you dedicated to following yesterday's money? And why are you telling me all these strange things? I mean, like, I never heard those wild ideas in college. About, I mean, the past being such a great and wonderful age, a time in history that was so simple compared with today's turmoil."

Slowly in a didactic tone, he said, "We learn from the past, both from its facts and its feelings." He went to his polished wooden desk. Opening a drawer, he pulled out a framed photograph. It was of Jack. In color. Lance held it up for each of them—father and sister—to admire. Her brother was in his Army dress uniform, ribbons ablaze. In a halting voice, Lance said, "He was a handsome young man. Have you ever seen this photo of your brother?"

"No," she said. Fleetingly, but deeply, Sara speculated that Jack might be the real reason she was here in Basel, the underlying, subliminal reason she had consented to accept the grant from the Institute to End War to begin her work on Kinkaid's project, to fly to Geneva to talk with Dr. Wolfe. And now here in Basel with her father. She was soon to be off to the Swiss Alps for... For what? She was uncertain. But in her pack, she reminded herself, she had a train ticket for the morrow.

Abruptly Lance told her, "I must go now. My driver will take you to the Hotel Euler for your stay tonight. Tomorrow he'll collect you and drive you to the train station." He smiled, shook her hand warmly, then hugged her, and she him as he said, "Good night, Sara." As she turned to leave, he added, "I'll see you when you've completed your research. Back here. Yes, definitely. You and I will have another reunion."

CHAPTER FIFTEEN:
CHATEAU ROUGEMONT

The excursion train, packed with skiers clutching skies, poles, and bulging backpacks—annoyed at the stop—waited impatiently as Sara disembarked at the tiny Rougemont station. Starting up again, the electric engine with its two cars in tow quickly picked up its pace, whisking its passengers toward the lifts and runs of Gstaad. Her pack clinging to her back, but ski-less, Sara waved a quick farewell to the people on the train she'd met.

Expectantly, curious as to what she would find ahead, Sara rapidly made her way along the platform until she found a "way out" sign pointing her up and out of the station. She felt a bit out of breath as she walked excitedly along a snow-packed road in the direction that her Internet map had indicated led to Chateau Rougemont. She remembered that the station sign showed "elevation 3,304 feet above sea level." Absently, she remarked to herself, "Indianapolis is only 600 feet" and thought no more about it as she took in the scenery with its snow, chalets, and evergreen trees—an idyllic Alpine landscape.

Not far off in the distance, across the snow-packed highway filled with winter vacationers journeying toward the ski slopes, Sara saw two silo-like spires rising into the bright blue noontime sky. She identified them as the spires she had seen in the picture of the chateau given to her by Dr. Wolfe. "They remind me of the grain silos back home in Indiana," she commented out loud to no one but herself and added, "Except these spires are pointing to heaven…."

Sara walked on toward her destination, then stopped short.

That sound. ever so different. From behind her. From the train depot came the energized sound of belching steam from an old-fashioned railroad engine.

As a little girl Sara recalled having seen a steam engine pulling an historic train along the soon-to-be-abandoned Monon Line north of Indianapolis. Puzzled, she turned and looked back toward the station.

83

The depot had metamorphosed into a Stick Style 19ᵗʰ century railroad station, albeit somewhat smaller than the modern one she had just left. Standing and puffing away on the rails in front of the station was not a modern train, but in its place a vintage steam train, not with an electric engine, for there were no overhead wires, nor was it pulling the modern excursion coaches like the one from which she had disembarked moments earlier. Instead, they were old-style carriages.

Sara recalled seeing similar coaches in the railroad museum in the restored 19ᵗʰ century Union Station in Indianapolis.

The weather was now turning colder.

From her pack she took out her goose down jacket, her mittens, her over-the-ears ski hat, now looking as if she were at the top of the lift and ready to descend at warp speed. Except no skis. No poles.

The sky was dark with heavy snow clouds. Just as quickly the snow was now coming down around her, covering her, and blowing into her face.

Red snow.

She caught a flake in her gloved hand. It was as red as the scarf she had wrapped around her shoulders to cover herself where her down jacket stopped and her delicate skin remained exposed to the sudden harsh mountain winter.

Looking back at the depot, she saw the dark smoke of railroad steam belching from the engine's stack, adding a dismal touch to the winter scene. The soot from the coal-burning engine gathered and hung over Rougemont as if it were an ominous warning from the guns of war.

In the distance, a few passengers de-trained from the old coaches. They carried no skis. No poles. No parkas or ski clothing. Wearing only wool greatcoats, leather gloves, and fur-covered hats. A servant was helping passengers with luggage, carrying their bags to a waiting wagon drawn by a team of horses. The passengers were climbing up onto the wagon and huddling together for warmth in the open conveyance. The driver called out before he urged the horses onward, "All aboard for Chateau Rougemont!"

Then overhead from off in the distance, coming closer, came an airplane with the whirring buzz of a propeller-driven craft.

Sara recalled the sound of the occasional private propeller plane landing or taking off from the little runway strip near her James Whitcomb Riley College campus.

Uh-oh. The plane's motor was sputtering as if uncertain of its course or its fate. In the West a plane was coming in low, smoke spewing from one of its two engines, a dark trail of certain doom. It was west of the chateau's silo-like towers, descending ominously toward a flat meadow deep in snow. The pilot seemed to be struggling with the controls. A beige cow, a lone cow, its hoofs foraging in the snow for some surviving grass, looked up. Startled, it tried to run, but which way? The cow was large. The plane now seemed small. The plane struck the side of the cow. Poor thing. Poor plane. From the impact, the craft bounded up and then pancaked down, hitting the snow with a flat almost splash, judging from the amount of snow billowing upward from the plane's impact.

Sara shook herself. Had she really witnessed a plane crash just now? Was this a dream? But no, there was a plane right there before her. With caution Sara approached the downed aircraft.

The insignia on the plane's side was a blue star in a white circle with squared-off protrusions extending from each side.

Sara recalled the World War II insignia of American planes she had seen in one of her history books.

The canopy of the plane rose, a hand and then an arm pushing it up from within. A struggling figure was trying to climb out. From below, another urged him on. That failing, with great effort, he pushed the first one up. Out now, and seemingly helpless, the man skidded down the side of the plane and hit the snow face down. He didn't move. The white snow around him turned red. The second figure extracted himself and jumped down to bend attentively over the first man, righting him in his arms, hoping to keep him alive.

Sara tried to move, for in her compassion she wanted to rush to their side and try somehow to help. Red snow fell around her. Red snow. She felt dizzy. She almost lost her balance. She was unable to pick up her feet and move toward the downed airplane. It was like a nightmare when you can't wake up, or move, or cry out. She shut her eyes, but no, her eyes were already closed to shut out the terror before her. She tried to open her eyes, but the vision of the crashed plane and the two pilots, one lying in the snow, the other bending over his companion froze in her mind. She couldn't think or move. It was as if she were frozen in the snowy scene, a manikin mandated to permanence in a Swiss Alpine winter scene. And what year was it anyway?

Then Sara heard the voice coming from behind calling her name, "Ms. Vogel?" It was a soft, cordial female voice. Young. Sara thought she heard a motor, this time the uneven putt-putt of a bike.

Turning to see who it was calling her name, Sara glimpsed a clear bucolic Alpine scene. No snow was falling. With confusion, doubt, and hope, she weakly responded, "Yes?"

A girl on a motorbike had pulled up. In perfect English, the girl said, "I've been sent by my grandfather, the chateau caretaker, to give you a ride. Herr Ellis is waiting to welcome you to Rougemont."

"You're—"

"—Melissa, Herr Ellis' granddaughter."

"But the plane?" Sara pointed toward the field. She looked. This time she saw no downed plane. No pilot helping his wounded companion. No smoke. No injured cow. Just winter snowpack, unstained by wreckage or blood. Worse, the few snow flurries now blowing around her were pure Swiss mountain white.

"Hop on," was Melissa's directive as she raced the impatient engine.

Pack on her back, Sara straddled the vehicle and glanced back over her shoulder at the station. No train waited. The depot was the one when she had arrived. "Ever get a steam engine here?" Sara asked.

Melissa said, "No."

"But I just saw one."

Melissa laughed. "You've come from sea level. You've probably got a touch of altitude sickness. It can cause delusions. Last time I remember a steam train going though here was a tour train for railroad buffs, and that was a long time ago. Hold on, off we go."

Distraught, Sara protested, "But what about the airplane in the field there in the snow?"

Melissa laughed again. "Granddad said you might be a little tired following your jet flight.

The bike sped up. They crossed the highway, dodging between cars and buses filled with skiers, skis, and pointed poles. "I'm going up tonight," Melissa said, gesturing with her head toward the Alpine slopes to the east.

Within moments they were droving past old church. Sara could tell its age from the architecture and patina on the wooden doors, windows, and headers. The stained glass windows were brilliantly colorful. In a loud voice, Melissa pointed and called out, "The chapel was built hundreds of years ago, the first church in Switzerland, or anywhere to be built by its own monks."

Before Sara could comment, the bike bounced across a row of cobblestones, passed beneath a crafted wooden archway, and entered a flagstone-paved courtyard. Looming ahead was the multi-storied Chateau Rougemont. Large wooden shutters flanking the many windows displayed the design Sara had seen in the pictures given her by Dr. Wolfe. The shutters were painted with irregular green bolts, like bursts of lightning. Against a white background, each bolt shot outward, indicating infinity, so she thought, or maybe the grandeur of the Swiss Alps. Painted high up on the side of the chateau, Sara saw a stylized rooster. She recalled Erika pointing to it in one of the photographs, suggesting it might be Chaucer's famed rooster, Chanticleer, watching over its wives inhabiting the chateau. Seeing the bird, Sara sensed the description was fitting. She wondered what had the cock witnessed? What did it know? What secrets might it, would it, reveal to her? Perhaps in its crowing. But she knew the rooster was just a painted image.

To her right, separate from the chateau, but still old, stretched a long single-storied gabled building. Sara surmised that it one time or another it must have quartered the servants who worked for the important people living in the chateau. Way back in time, the residents might have been royalty, people of society. During the war, they were the central bankers socializing together—the banking royalty, the BIS central bankers from each of the warring nations. And the servants who lived in this outlying building must have been the nameless seven who had been in service to the bankers. Sara would try to find out who the servants were that made up the chateau's staff during the war.

Jolting Sara from her reflections came Melissa's voice. "Ring the leather belt holding the string of sleigh bells. It's hanging beside the door on the right. My grandfather will get you settled in." Sara hopped off the bike as Melissa pointed eastward. "Gstaad," she said. "I'll just grab my skis, poles, and then I'm off to meet friends."

"But the airplane in the field?" Sara pointed. "Over there?"

Melissa looked at Sara and asked uncertainly, "You okay?" To Sara's silence, she replied, "Honey, there's no downed plane. Just look."

Sara did. Again. No plane. No pilot in the snow. No wounded or possibly dead airman sprawled by his side. What happened to the warplane that had been shot down? She turned back to Melissa, who had retrieved her skis and was hoisting them across her back. In one swift movement, Melissa kicked the start lever, and the bike, like a motivated Bernese Swiss Mountain Dog on a rescue mission, surged forward, its master steering.

CHAPTER SIXTEEN:
THE PROVENANCE

Left alone, Sara stood by the door, signed above in small letters "M. Ellis-Caretaker." Posted by the door was a free standing placard displaying an artist's drawing of the chateau in springtime. A row of flowering fruit trees blossomed along its façade, which faced the towering Alps. A narrative in French, German, and English, told about the chateau's centuries of history. There was no mention of the Bank for International Settlements being in residence during World War II. Sara studied the placard before jiggling the string of sleigh bells announcing her presence.

No response from inside.

Sara shook the bells again, harder this time and, in the ensuing silence, waited with patience growing into anxiety. Uncertain, given the on-going silence, she knocked gently on the worn wooden door. Nothing. Boldly, yet gently, she pushed against the door. Slowly it swung open, its hand-forged iron hinges creaking. Tiptoeing across the threshold, she entered and called softly, "Mr. Ellis" and waited to hear what she anticipated would surely be his responsive welcome.

Before stepping farther inside, Sara surveyed the décor of the interior. Lining the far wall were multiple bookshelves bursting with books. She wondered if they were photo albums, maybe scrapbooks? Maybe one of the folios contained the wartime servant's diary for which she was hoping to find. That is, if such a diary did exist and was actually here.

Her hopes were overridden by the sound from a small television set sitting atop a little table. The program was a drama of some sort, and she recognized some German words.

Entering the room, she saw an elderly man whom she judged to be really old. He was sitting in a rocking chair and facing the TV. She heard a snore. His head bobbed. Of course, he had fallen asleep while watching the TV.

On the wall, she saw a framed photograph faded from the patina of age. It captured the moment of two men shaking hands. One was smiling. Judging from their demeanor and dress, the picture was taken in an earlier time period. The smiling man looked American, judging from his attire. The other man was wearing a stiff collar and ancient-looking formal black tie and what was probably a wool morning coat, on which was pinned what appeared to be a German iron cross. He looked stern and ominous. Too serious. Not even the hint of a smile in conjunction with the presumably friendly handshake. Underneath the photograph she saw their names: Thomas McKittrick, United States, and Emil Puhl, Reichsbank. The names were familiar from those mentioned earlier by her professor. Sara knew if she looked in the envelope given to her by Erika Wolfe she would find their defined roles at the chateau. She'd do that later.

"Now," she told herself, "I must address the situation at hand." Warmed by the fire in the fireplace, her voice stronger, she tried to get the attention of the sleeping man, "Mr. Ellis," adding, "I'm Sara... Sara Vogel." Hearing no response, she raised her voice "Your granddaughter Melissa told me..."

Startled, the old man sat up and coughed. Eyes wide-open, he looked up at her standing over him, showing annoyance that she was blocking the TV. She worried at his disapproval.

"Closed," he blurted. "The chateau is closed up." He coughed again. "How'd you get in? Who are you?" Slowly, rather painfully, so it seemed to Sara, he rose from his chair, his face grimacing with the obvious discomfort from this sudden activity. "Sorry," he mumbled, "sciatica." Then he asked, "What did you say your name was? Did the owner send you? Otherwise, I'm not supposed to let anyone into the chateau. Her orders."

Sara began again, "My name's Sara Vogel. Your granddaughter..."

He interrupted, "Cute. My granddaughter... you, too. How old are you? Girls are cute these days... not like back then... those long dresses... few smiles..." He gestured at the framed photograph behind him. "Terrible days. The 1930s. The depression. The rise of Hitler. Some might say that, in hindsight, they were well defined years. Then the war came. Destroyed everything and everybody. Terrible. Awful times."

His mentioning the war brought back an image of the downed aircraft. Sara asked, "During the war, did many American planes crash land in Switzerland?"

Ellis nodded. "German, too."

"What became of the crews, the pilots?"

Ellis seemed to come more alive, beginning to act as if he were a professor in a classroom. "Interned by the Swiss for the duration of the war. That is, except when Allen Dulles intervened."

"John Foster's younger brother."

"You know about him?" After Sara said she had read about him, Ellis went on, "Allen Dulles was near here... in Bern—"

"—The Swiss capital."

After a confirming nod, Ellis said, "Recruited some of the downed American pilots for his own espionage—before he became head of the CIA after the war. Back then he was running his own personal spy network. You know, this place, especially right here in this chateau, was a beehive of spies, rumor, intrigue... If only we had more journals, memoirs, diaries..."

"More? Then you know of a wartime journal?" No reply. She asked, "Was it kept here? Perhaps by one of the seven servants?" She gestured at the bookshelves lining the far wall, adding, "Maybe left by the previous owners?"

"—You're Skip's granddaughter?"

Sara was surprised by his changing the subject. "Ah, no."

"Kinkaid, I mean."

"My professor at JWR College, Skip Kinkaid?"

"Of course. We go way back." He reiterated, "Melissa is my granddaughter."

"Yes, so she told me... minutes ago... said you knew I was coming."

Slowly he replied, "He—Skip, that is—got me this job after I retired. Not that I needed the income. I have my generous university pension. Skip's college is going broke." She said she knew that.

"He and I reconciled, you see, I forget when it was. We met one day and talked at length. I acknowledged that his take on the cause of wars was as legitimate as mine—it was an honest disagreement between history professionals lost in the jealous pride of the ivy-covered towers of academia. It got blown out of proportion. We each showed compassion, as I recall. Nice. Buried the hatchet, as they say. And it's not Mr. It's Dr. I've a PhD." He laughed. "Always been one up on old Skip as to our degrees."

Sara recalled her conversation with Kinkaid on that day several years ago when he told her his PhD story—the confrontation with his department head. Now she was talking to that department head. Pleased about their mending the rift, she tried to return to the subject of her reason for visiting the chateau. "Melissa said you knew I was—"

"—No one's allowed in the chateau, you know. It's all closed up, locked tight. I keep it that way. For the new owner, you know."

"Dr. Ellis, I'm not with the new owner." Sara wondered what importance current ownership meant for her World War II investigation. Could be a connection. Anyway, she asked, "But who is the new owner?"

Ignoring her question, he said, "There's not much here... Sara, you said?"

"Yes, Sara Vogel."

"Well, if you want to stay the night, go down the line to door number 7. I've a key here somewhere." He walked to a cabinet and opened a door. She saw clutches of keys hanging from hooks on the backside of the door. He searched for a moment, mumbling numbers, soon picking out a key with a brass number 7 hanging from it. He handed it to Sara.

She accepted the key and asked, "When is Melissa returning from her ski trip?" His gaze shifted back to the TV program. He didn't reply. She asked again about the journal to which he had so obliquely referred. "Was it written by one of the servants? Is it stowed in your bookcases, or is it hidden away somewhere in the chateau?" He ignored her question. Why doesn't he answer? Annoyed, she pressed. "Melissa?" Then she remembered the words from Pierre, her Geneva cab driver, and said, "Do you know Lena? I'm supposed to look her up in the village of Rougemont."

He turned and looked intently at Sara. "How do you know her?"

"Pierre told me—"

"—Yes, of course I know her. Actually I'm going to her place a little later."

"Her place?"

"It's a pub up over the Tourist Office." He returned his attention to the TV.

Sara puzzled as to what to do next. Then she asked, "Do you have a car?"

He nodded absently. "Outside in the courtyard."

"Can I go with you?" she added, "I've a message for Lena."

He didn't answer right away. Then reluctantly, she thought, he explained, "The pub—well, during the war I guess it was called a beer garden, but now we call it a pub—is left over from the war years when her mother ran it… named it after Lena." He looked Sara up and down, his eyes now much more interested in her than the TV drama. "You a dancer? They've only a few dancers these days… the dancing part of the club is almost defunct. Lena says women have too many other career choices these days that pay good money. Anyway, she says she's too busy running the pub—about the only decent place to eat hereabouts." He looked at her intently and said, "You'd be a good dancer, Sara." His smile lingered along with his inspecting gaze.

"Dr. Ellis, I'm not a dancer. I'm a researcher bent on a mission." Sara changed the subject, "Lena's German?"

"So's almost half the people here, the rest French. Speaking, that is." He added, "Most people are bi-lingual. Especially the local librarian in Rougemont. She's a friend, too… name's Elsa."

"She's been here a long time, too, like Lena?"

"I suppose so, yes, actually she told me so one day. Years." His voice tailed off, perhaps embarrassed, she thought. Then, "Tell you what, Sara, you stay here while I go to see Lena and have one of her Swiss cheese sandwiches. That's in case the new owner or her concierge shows up. Wouldn't do to have no one here."

"And what if they want to go inside the chateau? Where's the key so I can welcome them and let them in?"

"Oh, I don't know about that…"

"Why not?" She added, "It would look strange if I don't know where the key is stashed, and they want to go inside." She thought. "I'll say I'm your granddaughter, Melissa, and you've gone to town for some dinner."

He thought for a moment.

Sara reminded him, "The key to the chateau?"

He nodded. "Oh, yes." He walked back over to the cabinet and retrieved a key from the backside of the door and handed it to Sara. "It's for the rear door."

Sara nodded her thanks. To her surprise, she heard him say, "And you could tell them—that is, if the new owner comes—that you're a friend of the previous owners."

"Not the Tucks?" She said, "No, he passed away. So, who was the previous owner?"

Ellis said, "The Guths, Polly and John. They're from some town in New Hampshire. Elsa told me they bought the chateau from the heirs of President Herbert Hoover's friend. That would be William Hallam Tuck. She says Tuck was Hoover's man arranging massive food relief for starving Belgians right after World War I." He added, "Yes, and even after the last war, that is until Mr. Tuck died right here in the chateau… I think around 1966."

"How did the BIS?—"

"—Story is—"

"—Story, not fact?"

He sat back down in his chair with a sigh and looked at Sara. "You're too young to remember the 1930s."

"My father has told me some things about the 1930s." Sara looked at him quizzically. "What more should I know?" To Sara, Dr. Ellis seemed to be gathering his thoughts—like pulling dusty books from an archive—as he traveled back in time to what must seem, even to him as a history professor, a distant and murky past.

"You see, Sara, in those days—unlike today as I remember it, there were not nearly as many what we would call 'important' people in society. Back home in the U.S. and Europe, this small group of influential people—mostly men—all knew each other…"

"All male?"

"Yes, as I said, maybe not a hundred percent…"

"Ninety?"

Another nod. "At least." He went on. "They were the men running businesses, governments, charities, states. Also the military."

"So, what does that mean?"

Ellis stood and gestured toward the chateau. "When problems developed in government, like at the beginning of the Second World War, these men talked to each other as if they were back in college at some fraternity party, or else they saw themselves as players on the college football team. Your see, Mr. Tuck was Thomas McKittrick's personal friend. So, when McKittrick became head of the BIS at the outbreak of the war, he telephoned Tuck, telling him they had to move the BIS headquarters out of Basel as the Germans might well invade the Swiss lowlands. Tuck is supposed to have said to

McKittrick, 'y'all can go to my chateau up there in the Alps at Rougemont. You and your fellow bankers will be safe there.' And that's what happened."

Sara took out her laptop and made notes of the story while Ellis watched her fingers caress the keyboard. She asked, "After the war, what happened to the ownership? I mean, you said there is a new owner."

"Well, after Tuck died, the Guths bought the place. That was after the big fire that devastated the chateau, after which Tuck's family lovingly restored the Medieval building to its original grandeur."

"When was that?"

"In the late 1970s, so Elsa told me. The old place was put back to what it had been during the war. That's the building you see today."

Sara made more notes on her laptop and asked, "But who is the new owner?"

Admiring her with a smile, Ellis quipped, "You are a curious young lady." Sara waited. He said, "One of the wealthiest women in Italy and the world, so I read in that issue of *Vanity Fair* in the bookcase over there. She's the controversial heiress to the fabulous Fiat fortune." He grew quiet. Soon he added, "Not a woman you want to cross. That's why I've been hired to watch over the place."

Sara asked herself if Erika Wolfe might know this new owner. She wondered if Switzerland today was like America in the 1930s. A time when the important people in the world all knew each other. Probably no longer the case, Sara suggested to herself, either because there were so many rich and important people in Switzerland and around the world, or there were simply too many resorts and clubs to belong to. Or perhaps they were all competing to be highlighted on the most wealthy media list that tabulated personal assets and ranked the rich. Must be nice, or fun, or worrisome to be rich and important. Which? Sara asked herself.

CHAPTER SEVENTEEN:
INSIDE THE CHATEAU

Entering room number 7 in the servants' quarters building, Sara found a small cot, several folded blankets, a well-used wood stove with lots of ashes, and years of dust. An adequate temporary place for her, Sara thought as she sneezed. She found a rag and cleared away some of the dust and set her stuff on a bare wooden table.

On her way to number 7, she had spotted Ellis' car parked in the courtyard. She waited until she heard the car's motor start, telling her he was leaving for town. Then she began her inspection walk of the chateau. She followed a path that led her around the building, allowing the opportunity to admire the architecture of the Medieval structure.

Her mind traveled back in time to the 15th century. She absorbed the ambiance of the place, recalling the historic description on the placard outside Ellis's door. The chateau faced the Alps to the south across intervening fields. One of the fields must be where she had heard and seen the World War II warplane come down with the drama of its two escaping airmen. Now, there was no cow, no plane, no pilots, and the fields were blanketed with undisturbed pure white snow. Had the pilots, if they survived, been interned by the Swiss? Or gone to Bern to work as spies for the head American wartime sleuth, Allen Dulles?

Sara continued on the lightly trodden snow along a faint path. In circling the chateau, she speculated about the events the Medieval people had witnessed... oh, so many years ago. She imagined knights in their armor with lances riding spirited horses... rugged, handsome, fierce knights, idealized knights. She saw beautiful ladies in elegant attire riding sidesaddle on their tame horses. Running loose scampered little children, the boys' eyes wide as they admired the knights, the little girls smiling up at the ladies as they rode past. A king, or perhaps he was a prince, up on an elegant white steed, trotted by, his crown glistening in the sunlight, the medley of royalty's riches eliciting loud cheers and salutary waves from the local artisans manning their stalls in the adjacent market place. What a glorious, colorful time in history Medieval pageants must have been for those people. Everything was in its place. Everybody had their prescribed role that the culture decreed for them.

Sara thought about her father glorifying the 1930s as a structured and satisfying time period when everything and everybody fit into the socially prescribed role. Yet, as she thought more about those past ages, she began to question both her own bucolic idealism and that of her father. What was important to those people in their lives? Their children? Their religion? Maybe just survival? Or simply happiness and what might have been called prosperity in their time? What was becoming important in her life? For sure, she wasn't fitting herself into a role, a societal slot, or was she? Yearning for deeper understanding of life, then and now, and of herself, Sara walked on, comfortable joining in the embrace of the ambiance of the historic Medieval chateau with its painted rooster watching over.

Around the next corner, she found herself back on the side closest to the gabled building—the servants' quarters. There she saw what she presumed to be the chateau's rear door, almost hidden down a short staircase. It must have been the servants' entrance. Surely not the main entrance. Why did Ellis not give her the key to the main entry doors on the Alps side of the chateau? A few paces back, she had passed those two elegant wooden doors. Wouldn't those doors be more fitting for the new owners to enter should they arrive? That is, if they ever did arrive. And when would that be... imminent tonight... or not at all?

She tried the rear door key. It worked. The door creaked open. With anticipation and excitement, Sara entered Chateau Rougemont. Passing through the doorway, she suddenly sensed she was privy to secrets. But what secrets awaited her? Secrets about the war? The BIS bank? The central bankers and their wives? Her skin tingled. Suddenly she wanted to flee. Was she intruding into a past time? A closed time that was over and done with? Such as the Medieval life she had just visualized taking place in the ancient community around the chateau. Pausing only momentarily, Sara realized this was her opportunity to explore. To sense more. Isn't this what historians do?

Discover things that bring the past to life?

In the vastness of the chateau's interior, a feeling of being incredibly alone overcame Sara. It was weird. But then, as she stepped across the broad planks of the wooden floor, she sensed the presence of someone, maybe more than one person. She saw no other human being, yet she was sure she heard a muffled voice. A male?

Venturing forward, an image of what must be her grandfather came to her. He had been a lesser member of German royalty. Jack had told her about him. He had lived in Germany in the 1930's. He had sensed danger and fled the Nazis. Could it possibly be his presence—his spirit—that she felt? Was her grandfather Lance's father? Yet he said he didn't know about his father. Was that who was somehow here with her at this moment in Chateau Rougemont? Her grandfather's spirit? Whatever did that word mean to her? "Spirit." Grandfather's name had been von Reichard, but in Germany, he had changed it to Vogel. By the time he came here, if indeed this is where he did come, he was known as Herr Vogel. With blind hope, Sara called out, "Grossfather Vogel..." And then again. In return, only silence. Except for that same muffled voice coming from somewhere.

Apprehensive, even fearful in the fading light of early evening dusk, Sara crept farther through the chateau. There was no furniture, only sterile blank walls, some rooms with old wallpaper, some rooms painted one color, other walls and rooms in different colors. She found the central stairway and, afraid she might disturb something or someone, tiptoed up the wooden steps. Had she heard a spirit from long ago, a ghost of some former inhabitant? On the next floor, she felt the same vacant, lonely feeling. And on the floor above it the same. Upward to the top, the same. A hollowness. A sense of a vast void. The interiors had been stripped of furniture, paintings, anything to afford an interior character befitting the chateau's heritage. The former owners had taken everything away. So, where could be that diary or memoir for which she was looking? It must be gone, non-existent, at least it was not here in the chateau. Sara was overcome with the sensation she was not alone. Yet she felt alone, by herself in the vast empty Chateau Rougemont.

Having watched the people get off the train at the old station and climb onto the horse-drawn wagon, Sara wondered where were those people. Well, obviously they weren't here inside the chateau, any more than the servant helping them with their luggage.

In the silence, for now she heard no voices, Sara found her mind returning to the earlier scene at the train depot—only it hadn't been today's depot, but rather one from years ago. Nor had the people been dressed in contemporary clothing. She remembered, too, the downed aircraft and the two airmen in uniform in the falling red snow. It had been red hadn't it? But these scenes, Sara realized, with growing alarm, were not in her lifetime. No, she realized, she had witnessed events from years ago. How many years? She was not interested in doing the math, nor in experiencing anxiety that might border on panic.

Sara turned toward the stairs she had most recently climbed and made a hasty retreat down to the main floor. With her heart beating so rapidly she could hear it, she elected to head back to the servants' entrance, anticipating the relief she would feel with her imminent exit.

But wait! Who was that? Someone—a man—was standing right there in front of the rear door. For sure, it must be, at least on her part. But his? And was he her neighbor from Indianapolis—how many years removed? He looked like the photograph—given a few years of growing up—that had disappeared from her neighbor's photo album that day when his mother was showing her pictures of her son.

Sara looked again at the exit door. He was gone.

The vacant doorway stared at her, and she at it. Uncertain, Sara stood there, frozen. Then she looked around, even turned to see behind her. No one. First in a muffled voice, then more loudly, she voiced her friendly—yes she had made her voice sound friendly, hadn't she? She called, "Captain Richards... I'm Sara Vogel" Speculating on him and on herself, she wanted to say, "from the house next door to your parents." But all she could say was, "Are you here? Are you hurt? Injured from the crash?" She waited. "Please, Captain Richards, answer me."

From outside, from overhead. She thought she heard a rooster's crow. Was it Chanticleer? The bird seemed to be calling out in a melodious bird sentence. But it wasn't dawn. A distant raven sounded, perhaps in reply. Answering? Agreeing?

Sara's fright returned in the now almost dark, and she wanted to escape, Sara took the stairs two at a time. She saw the path and ran along it toward number 7. The exertion stimulated her mind. She recalled her father's statements about his description of his presumed idyllic 1930s. Maybe she had listened too intently to him, imagining those long-ago times as he had gone on to describe them. Or, as the next thought seized her, had she, his daughter, inherited some weird sixth sense of time and place from him and also possibly from her mother, perhaps a perspective that idolized history? Was she reliving the past, re-experiencing the war years? Was she, Sara Vogel, time traveling? Was that even possible? As she ran, she recalled her mother's absorption with the idea of clairvoyance and her continuous efforts to talk to her ancestors. Sara worried, or did she hope, that her parents' traits were hers? Was that an explanation for her seeing the events of this day? Maybe…

As Sara ran back along the path, she remembered reading a fellow student's essay speculating, no, actually claiming the feasibility of time travel. She recalled the student had something of a reputation as a science fiction freak. Now, reconsidering the matter, Sara wondered, she wondered if he indeed might be an imaginative scientist. She tried to recall what he had written. Yes, something about "wormholes" in outer space—a sense of time that allowed anyone to connect to what happened in different time periods in history's depths. Further, he had argued that, if you allowed yourself to view time as a circular progression rather than in a straight lineal concept, you would be liberated from the prevailing thinking about the irrevocable chronological passage of time. For time would circle around. If you made that mindful leap, he had averred, you could connect anywhere within this time circle. It would be, he had explained, like joining a line of dancers by breaking into their human chain and singing along with them in harmony without disrupting their merriment. Sara chuckled, albeit briefly, telling herself that back home in Indiana there were actually some original thinkers. Was his idea true science? Or wild imagination? She pondered the question as she approached the servants' quarters. She wished she had talked more to this presumably "wacky" fellow student. For wasn't she herself here in Rougemont running through one of the "wormholes" of time? A dancing chain that she had joined. Without jolting those enjoying the musical progression, or disturbing its choreography.

Ellis's car had not returned. Outside number 7, Sara began to shiver in the cold. She changed her mind and hurried to the caretaker's door. As earlier, it opened. Entering, she welcomed the residual interior warmth radiating from the fading coal in the fireplace. She added a couple of chunks of the black mineral and plunked down wearily in Ellis's favorite chair, waiting for the resurging blaze to warm her as she tried to sort out the day's amazing events.

CHAPTER EIGHTEEN:
THE BOOKCASE

Sitting there, warming herself, waiting for the return of Dr. Ellis, relishing this time of solitude and the opportunity to reflect, Sara asked herself what she would say to the retired professor when he did return. Or would she, once warmed from the fire, simply leave for her night in number 7? Pondering, Sara surveyed the cluttered room of the retired professor, Chateau Rougemont's resident caretaker.

No longer distracted by the now-dark TV, she saw additional framed photographs on the walls. She judged each to be of similar vintage as the one she had seen earlier above Ellis's chair. She toured the room. Each photograph was labeled with the names of the men, along with the title of their central bank and its country of origin. Sara noted their names and wished the chateau had Internet access so that when she returned to her number 7 and turned on her computer she could access the Institute to End War's special search engine and read about each of these World War II BIS men. Had they been living here, sending gold around the world and eventually to… to where? To Berlin? Were they players on a bloody chessboard, each clutching a cache of gold ingots while socializing with other world bankers and their wives over cocktails?

Sara walked over to a shelf in the taller bookcase. One by one, she examined each of the folios. Reading each typewritten title, she hoped against hope to come across the rumored wartime memoir or diary written by one of the seven servants. The first folio contained maps of the canton; another, photographs of historic buildings in the town of Rougemont; another, a collection of both vintage and newer photographs of skiers in various time periods, back then and more recently, posing on the slopes at Gstaad. Amazed at the past, she said out loud, "Look at those old wooden skis, and their old fashioned clothes."

In another folio were photos depicting the chateau down through the years—exterior shots, some likely older were in black and white, while those more recent were in color. The next folio displayed photographs of the interior décor, each marked by the floor. Sara realized that the chateau had been filled with beautiful antiques, its walls decorated with original art—oils and watercolors—along with what she thought were old masters. Sculptures were displayed on pedestals. Some were cast in bronze, others obviously carved marble. Perusing the photos, Sara admired the luxury of the chateau's opulent antique collections. The previous owners were obviously wealthy. Under their direction, the chateau had been a virtual museum.

Unfortunately, she felt, the building had been allowed to revert to an unwelcome emptiness. The void of the chateau's interior décor represented a lost history. Pining for its earlier elegant times, she lamented the passing of the historic charm of the chateau. Only the architecture remained as a testament to the Middle Ages.

A smaller, rather fragile looking folio had been tucked into the shelf, visible only when she pulled out the last and largest book. The smaller book was a bound compendium of wildflower photos. In the front, still loosely clinging to the binding of the spine, the title page was as dog-eared as the photographs of flowers with their written descriptions, many sheets having separated from the little book's binding. The title page said the book, with its many photographs, had been compiled by Martin Nils. He was extolled as a village pastor in what must have been a nearby community. The publication date was 1938. The publisher was in Dresden. The text was in German. Flipping through the photos, she admired the Alpine flowers, expressive in their captivating display of beauty.

The last of the folios, larger than the rest, was not identified, its loose sheets handwritten. Excitedly, Sara asked herself if this was the diary or memoir for which she was searching? The writer had beautiful penmanship, but it was in old-fashioned German script. Sara wished she had studied German as her second language at JWR instead of devoting so many semester hours to Spanish.

From outside she heard the engine of an arriving car. Dr. Ellis came in, looked at her and said, "So, you're still here."

Sara smiled. "Yes, I am. No one came while you were away." Then she asked, "Dr. Ellis, can I get on the Internet here?"

Hanging up his jacket and rubbing his hands together in front of the coal fire, he said, "No, not here. But Lena has the Internet... at her pub."

Sara felt relief. "So, I can get on the Internet there." She thought about Lena being German. "She must read German? Translate, I mean."

"Yes, I suppose so. If she's too busy, then Elsa, our librarian, can. She's good at languages. What do you need to translate?"

She showed him the folio with the loose sheets and the precise penmanship. Sara held up the little picture book of wildflowers and said, "Isn't this beautiful!"

Dr. Ellis smiled and with justification in his voice, said, "I saved them from the clutches of the movers."

"Why?"

"They may have historic value. Having been a scholar ll my life, I hate to throw away what might be primary source material. To do so, as I always told my students, is to discard a legacy. In this case, the chateau's valuable heritage. Someday they might turn out to be an important bit of history. I can read enough German to realize that this diary, and that's what it is, might be of interest to some scholar someday."

"I can't tell you how glad I am that you did. They're of great interest to me, now, today. But I can't make head or tails of the old German script."

"Okay, Sara. We'll go to Lena's in the morning. If she doesn't have time to help you, she'll introduce you to Elsa—Lena calls her Ellie—our Rougemont librarian. She may be able to help. Today I told Lena about you."

"What did you say?"

"That you're my friend Skip's granddaughter. Now, if you will excuse me, young lady, given my age, I'm going to bed."

*   *   *

Safely back in number 7, Sara couldn't sleep, thinking about the diary. And, as well, her encounter with the ghost of the World War II pilot who had lived next door to her parents' house in Indianapolis. What a night! She had so much to write about. Only she would be the one to write this story, her story. It would be like an assignment back in college. But, she reminded herself, she was out of college now. She was in the real world. Her composition was to be real writing. It would be her very own female gender gaze.

CHAPTER NINETEEN:
LENA'S PUB

Driving in Dr. Ellis' car, Sara had asked, "How long has Lena's Pub been in Rougemont?"

"Oh, a long time. Goes back before the war, I'm told. Then it was a... ah... what might be called today 'a gentlemen's club.' Lena told me her mother started it as a wartime club after she fled Germany in the 1930s."

"From where in Germany?"

"Munich, I think her mother may have been flirting with the White Rose group and feared for her safety. But you are an inquisitive young woman."

"I'm a female historian. Curiosity is a prerequisite."

"Here we are. Follow me up the stairs."

Sara realized patrons must already know the location of Lena's Pub, for it wasn't signposted or lit by a neon sign. In fact, like the location of the BIS in Basel in the early years of World War II, or so Erika Wolfe had described, only a select few bankers knew its location—unidentified as it was in an old hotel above a chocolate shop. She had asked Erika why the bank had such a clandestine location... her question being shrugged off as inconsequential to her assignment. Was the bank's mission, Sara asked herself, so secret that its bankers didn't want anyone to know of its location, let alone its existence? But the BIS was a known quantity. Known by how many? In the media? People in general? By the politicians in the USA? And those in other countries? Sara reasoned, her mission was to unearth a bundle of answers. That is, if they did exist.

Sara followed Dr. Ellis up the staircase that clung to the exterior of the Rougemont Tourist Office, which itself was up a hill rising behind and overlooking the railroad station.

*   *   *

Upon their arrival, Lena hugged Ellis perfunctorily, so Sara surmised. He tried to introduce Sara. "This is... well, she's the granddaughter of—"

"—I'm Sara Vogel, Lance Vogel's daughter. I'm here in Rougemont to—"

"—Vogel?"

Sara nodded. "Pierre in Basel said to—"

"—How do you know him?"

"He drove my taxi. He said to look you up."

Lena held up her hand, palm toward Sara. "Wait. Back up. Are you looking to dance here?"

"Oh, no, not at all. I'm researching—"

"—Aren't we all?" Lena laughed, adding, "Men..."

Sara surveyed Lena. She looked German, whatever that might suggest, but that's what Sara saw. Had Lena had a facelift? Yes, Sara concluded. But she asked herself, what did that matter to her research assignment? To Sara, Lena appeared callous with the look and manner of street-smart experience. However, Sara detected a certain grace and openness. Her eyes were as green as Sara envisioned these Alpine foothills to be in springtime. Her wavy hair was as white as the snow now covering the nearby Alps. Right off, Sara sensed a certain comfort being in Lena's presence. She said, "Pierre told me you are German and smart." And then she wondered why she said those words and wished she'd been more cordial and less effusive.

Lena laughed again. Smiling benevolently, she said, "How old are you, Ms. Vogel?"

"Old enough to dance here but, of course, not wanting to. Old enough to have a serious research and writing job, which I am currently pursuing."

"Tell me, Sara, what is this so-serious job?"

"I'm doing research on World War II and the role played by the BIS bankers here in Rougemont. And at the chateau. I'm trying to learn what I can about how and why wars are financed." In the ensuing silence, Sara waited as both Lena and Dr. Ellis looked at her, perhaps, she worried, in condescending disbelief, given her age. "And, she hastened to add, now I need a translator, Old German to Modern English."

Lena nodded, "For sure we can find you a translator. World War II was a long time ago. Yes, the world's central bankers were here, supposedly moving gold back and forth between their central banks. And especially to Berlin..." Lena shook her head, which Sara interpreted as a negative judgment.

In the ensuing silence, Lena studied Sara. "Has Vogel always been your name?"

"Why do you ask?"

"I thought so." Lena said softly to herself, then motioned for Sara to follow her. "We need to have a serious conversation, young lady. "In my office. Dr. Ellis will wait, won't you?" As if he didn't mind being excluded from the conversation, he said, "I'm afraid I can't. I need to get back to the chateau in case the new owners show up."

*   *   *

In her office, Lena pointed to a wall where timeworn photographs of women dancers were hung. "This was the place back during World War II—the time you're wanting to look into. It was a dance hall then. These days we're a pub. Only occasionally on Saturday nights after the tourist office closes, do we have dancers with Swiss music. Young women have so many more opportunities today to find work and, yes, pursue careers, as you are doing. Lena looked intently at Sara. "So, Sara Vogel, young American historical researcher, tell me about yourself."

Sara explained how she had taken on her college professor's research project. She confided to Lena that her career objective was to become a creditable woman historian along the lines of Barbara Tuchman and Jane Appleby but with more emphasis on women in history.

Lena said, "I don't have time to read much, but Ellie mentioned reading Tuchman."

Sara recited, "Guns of August," and then watched Lena closely as she told her about viewing the murals at the Institute to End War in Geneva.

Lena pressed Sara, "You've changed your name to Vogel?"

Hesitatingly Sara said, "No, not me. I didn't."

"Not your father either? I'm correct in that?"

Sara nodded. "My brother Jack, before he was killed in Afghanistan, told me that my grandfather changed our family name in fear of the Nazis. Grandfather was worried about having Jewish ancestors, and the Nazis were closing in. Apparently it worked, for he was able to escape Germany. Jack's guess was that he knew another royal like himself, who was already here."

"What was your grandfather's name?"

"Von Reichard."

Lena's whistle reflected her out-of-the-blue surprise. Yet, Sara sensed, Lena had a pre-knowledge that seemed to somehow mitigate her whistle. Sara reacted by saying, "You're taken aback, but not that surprised. Why?"

Lena grasped Sara's hand. "I've never believed in Extra Sensory Perception. That is, until now... only sort of..."

"I don't understand."

"Let me tell you something. But first let's share a Swiss custom." Lena opened the cabinet behind her desk. From a mini refrigerator, she pulled out a tall greenish bottle. "Swiss Neuchatel," she announced. Extracting a corkscrew, she decanted the wine and poured two glasses. She toasted softly, gesturing with emphasis, "Prosit!"

Her glass touching Lena's, Sara said, "My mother believes in clairvoyance."

"And your father?"

"He's a banker with today's BIS in Basel. I visited him on my way here. I think he does experience a sort of ESP."

Lena sipped her wine and said, "World War II may be long done with, but it is not over with."

Sara suggested, "Memories?"

Lena said, "Yes, memories of that war—they fill this place. Memories shared with me by my mother, and others when I was younger. "You see, Sara, the value—the amount—of gold that flowed through here was enormous. Not physically, but by orders of the world's central bankers." She pointed downward. "Right here. They're gone now... dead. All of them, I would presume. But their legacy, maybe even their presence lingers inside the chateau. The war created many troubled spirits."

Sara recalled the voices she'd heard the night before. It made her shiver with apprehension. She asked, "On Dr. Ellis' wall are photos of the BIS bankers. Where are their wives and children—no photos of them." She mused, "Or even grandchildren? They were here, too, weren't they?"

Lena said, "Yes. But in those days women were less visible outside their own circles. It was a man's world. Yet wives and children did live here in the chateau with their husbands."

"How do you know?"

"My mother used to talk about those days."

"Tell me... please."

Lena related, "She started the club here after she got out of Germany. She fled just in time. By then, young blond Aryan women such as my mother were being recruited, well, really forced to join a baby factory where they would be officially paired with the best of German males to produce physically conforming children that would perpetuate the so-called super race. To refuse, you could be carted away by the Gestapo and incarcerated with others they suspected of being dissidents, such as Socialists, Communists, homosexuals, gypsies, or Jews."

"Was your mother...?"

"She was a member of lesser German royalty. But she broke with her class and, trying to fulfill her patriotism to Germany and its people, she told me she became a union organizer. She believed that unions protect peoples' working rights and assure their health care. She confided to me that she flirted with Communists. She was on the verge of joining the White Rose Society, but with Hitler cracking down on everyone who didn't toe his line—dissidents—she fled her homeland and came here to Rougemont. She met women who were beating a retreat from France at the time of the French military defeat. Vaud, our cantonal division of Switzerland stretching from the other side of Chateau d/Ox up beyond Gstaad became a refuge for a host of refugees from all over Europe. Some of them became dancers here. A few knew the Can-Can and the Oo-la-la and the *je ne sais quoi*." Lena pointed. "Those are their pictures. They were beautiful, weren't they?"

"Your mother... she's..."

"Died, of course. Years ago. By then I was running this place. It was a dance hall, or gentlemen's club, as people called it—right here in this location. It was a magnet for refugees. One man was a refugee from Germany and a royal." She paused, perhaps for effect, Sara thought. Then Lena continued, "Later... after the war... I was born... he was my father."

Sara puzzled. "How did you know about my name?"

"You said you were Lance's daughter. Tell me, where was he born?"

Sara was slow to respond. "I guess... well, I don't really know."

"How old is he?"

"Again, I don't know... he's old, though."

"I do know."

Sara said, "You do? How?" Confused, she said, "How do you know about my father?"

Lena smiled. "Sara, there was a boy named Lancelot born right here in Rougemont in 1946..." Lena waited, allowing the information to register. Then she said slowly, "This boy was... Is... my older brother, by three years. My father's name was Vogel, too. My mother kept her name, as I did."

"Married?"

"I never knew for sure. My mother was evasive on the question." Lena paused and then went on, "When I was still very young, my father (your grandfather) left with his son. My mother said he'd tried going back to Germany, but soon became disillusioned and went to America. He was going to settle with other Germans he knew. He had read books by our German cowboy author, Karl May, and wanted to live in a place he thought had Indians. Where are you from, Sara? Is it one of those places?"

"I'm from Indiana. No Indians, but quite a few Germans."

Lena went on with her story. "As I said, Mr. Vogel, your grandfather, deserted me and my mother, taking little Lance with him. Mother was left on her own running the club. As time passed, I observed and learned, and I began helping out. We managed somehow to survive. It's a pub today, and it's still hard work." She reflected. "No business is easy."

"Did your father ever write?"

Belligerently, so Sara thought, Lena said, "We never heard from him. Mother told me once that she heard he had passed away." Lena looked hard at Sara, a stare that startled Sara. "And now... you... you say this Lance Vogel, a man who is my brother, is your father?" She reflected for a moment. "You know, I don't believe you." Lena's face tightened into a scowl. "I can't believe you." Her voice rose, "I mustn't allow myself to believe you, if it weren't so preposterous."

Sara reached into her pack and handed Lena her passport. Opening the official document, she pointed to her place and date of birth and then to her state of residency. She showed her the official Institute to End War's ID card given to her by Dr. Wolfe, attesting to "Sara Vogel's" affiliation with the Institute. "I'm as shocked as you, Lena. But you and I must believe each other."

As if experiencing an unwelcome epiphany, Lena said, "Sara, to survive this life of mine, I came to not think much about men beyond the surface. I learned to hate my father for deserting me and my mother. My hate for him became my reason for living, for my continuing, even years after the war was over, to run this club. I worked hard to bilk the lecherous young and old men who came in here. I viewed each of them as if he was my cruel father, and with each and every one of them who came with their selfish self-satisfying biological urge—male drive dominating their mind, I felt I was getting back at my father by milking them of their money. I got my revenge, I guess." Lena's voice sounded bitter and her scowl increased. She soon began to cry.

Sara moved close to Lena. Lovingly, she put her arm around the white-haired woman and said, "Lena, I must be your niece, and you my aunt. I'm so happy we're meeting."

Lena took out her linen handkerchief and dabbed at her moist eyes. "You're the only good thing that has ever come from having a long-lost brother."

Moved, Sara said, "All so unexpected when I came here."

Lena made a show of offering Sara a handkerchief, which Sara readily accepted. This made them both laugh in spite of their tears as they, in their own way, acknowledged their newly discovered family relationship.

CHAPTER TWENTY:
FAMILY

After a long silence, simply sitting there, being together, sipping their wine—unspoken emotions expressing what otherwise might turn out to be shallow and failed words—Lena said, "Sara, now you must tell me what it is you want help with."

Eagerly Sara replied, "The translation of this diary." She extracted the folio from her pack and showed Lena. "I found these papers in Dr. Ellis's bookcase. Handwritten in German. I'm hoping to learn more about the lives of the bankers and their families who lived here during the war. I'm hoping they tell about their lives."

Lena looked at a few sheets, examining the handwriting. "You need them translated?" More a statement than a question, Sara thought as she nodded. Lena said, "Most people here are bilingual—French, German, some Italian, most English, even Romansch speakers in remote mountain valleys—the most ancient of Swiss languages. This is a country of many tongues. Trick is to find someone with time to devote to your folio."

Lena asked Sara, "How much can you pay?" Lena sorted through some of the sheets. "There's a lot of work here, and the penmanship seems to change, too. One or two writers, or one more hurried, as time passes, maybe under time pressure."

Sara hadn't thought about paying anyone. But now, given the number of folio pages, she got a glimpse of the amount of work and time that translation would surely require. She remembered her special ATM card with access to the Institute's private Swiss bank account. She said, "Okay, yes, I can pay, I mean, I will pay."

Lena nodded. "Our librarian, Elsa, may be able to do the work. However, she has leanings that might be described as fascist, in case that troubles you."

"Well, the diary was written years ago. Her present political views don't matter, I guess. May I talk to her?"

"She's at the library. It's next to the Tourist Office. I'll go see. Give me a few minutes." Lena left the office and soon returned with an older woman, How old? Lena introduced her as Elsa, "really Ellie, our town librarian," and laughed, "and this is Sara." Right away, Sara was distracted by Elsa's good looks. Perhaps she had been a dancer before becoming a librarian. Excessive makeup, more than Sara would ever apply, but what difference did any of this description make, Sara asked herself, so long as Elsa would translate the folio.

Lena said, "Show Ellie the diaries."

Sara handed the folio to Ellie, noticing the smooth skin of her hands. She must use lots of lotion. So, why is that significant? Sara asked herself.

"It is a diary all right," Ellie said after perusing a few sheets. "It begins here in Rougemont in 1941."

Sara said, "That was after the BIS left its clandestine headquarters over the chocolate shop in Basel... and after they had given up on the Hotel du Parc in Chateau D/Ox in 1940... and left Basel to relocate here for the duration of the war."

Lena said, "So my mother once told me."

Ellie said, "Let's see how many pages there are." She started counting but soon gave up. "Obviously a lot." She looked at Sara and said, "I'd expect to be paid a fee, starting up front. You see, as librarian here I do get requests from various embassies in Bern to do translations for tourists, business people, and officials."

Sara thought she might be calculating the number of pages and multiplying by the number of hours of work per page that might be needed. Ellie asked, "How soon do you want me to start and when do you need me to get through the folio?"

Sara stumbled, "Well, beginning soon. It is my assignment, and I am under the gun to complete it as soon as possible." Sara reminded herself that Dr. Wolfe had not set a deadline for completion. Nevertheless, she asked herself how long did she want to remain here when she was due to start graduate school.

To Sara, Ellie's timing question came across as curt, but, Sara concluded, was business-like. With emphasis, Ellie smiled. "I'll be using my mind. Minds ought to be worth something special, don't you think?"

Sara asked, "Ellie, are you German?"

"Does ethnicity make a difference? Whether I'm German or Russian or whatever makes no difference in translation." Sara welcomed Ellie's next more germane-to-the-task statement. "Sara, you are offering me an historic peek back into the days of Nazi Germany, which I welcome, and am delighted to take on such an assignment."

Lena hurriedly said, "As I mentioned, Ellie and I don't always agree."

Sara said, "Ellie, do you welcome those days of old?"

"Well, not really, other than I think what is called 'the corporate state' is a system of government that offers a high level of stability. Most people want society to be stable, with jobs, paid vacations, and happiness for their children and grandchildren. Don't you think so?"

Sara said, "Like in the 1930s?"

Ellie smiled, rather to her self, Sara thought, and then went to a small shelf almost hidden in a corner of her library. Reaching in, she pulled out a leather book and dusted it with a towel. "I think you will want to read this."

"What is it?"

Ellie said, "Another diary. One of the girls working here during the war kept it. She writes about her life. It'll give you a feeling for those days. It's short but punchy."

"Who was the girl?"

"A German girl who spoke English. She was in school here in Switzerland. She didn't want to return to the Fatherland after the war started, although her parents stayed in Germany. From letters from her parents and from the men she met here in the club, many of them German, she tells about life during the war."

Sara said, "Thank you, Ellie, Erika told me such a diary might be here. It's been on my list to find, and now you're handing it to me."

Lena said, "Sara, maybe you want to read this before Ellie begins her translation."

"Yes, but there's no need to wait on translating the servant's diary."

Ellie said, "You will pay me in Swiss francs, of course, I assume."

"Of course. Swiss francs. How many?"

Ellie didn't hesitate. "Fifty an hour... cash, of course. That's so our Swiss librarian's union won't know, nor will the taxing authorities find out."

"Seems fair," Sara told her. She thought the tone of Ellie's voice was more asking than demanding. But since she would withdraw cash today… there must be an ATM downstairs in the tourist office… using the Institute's special card, why not? But how many hours would it take for she and Ellie to read through the diaries? That question remained in Sara's mind. She could try to negotiate Ellie's fee, but why?

Ellie said, "It has to be in the evening, late evening after dinner. I must feed Gerard, my invalid husband, and then I have to wash up."

It wasn't her money. So, yes, if her research project, for which she had come all this distance, was to move forward, she would need to agree to Ellie's terms. She did so by smiling as sweetly as she could. In a statement that left no room for discussion, she said, "Tomorrow… in the evening… we'll begin."

Ellie said, "Yes, let's get on with it."

Lena said, "11 PM in Ellie's library."

Ellie said, "Leave your folio with me and I'll take a quick run through. Meanwhile, Sara, look through this diary." She handed the German girl's little leather diary to Sara.

Sara asked, "Do you have a photocopy machine? I need to return the original folio sheets to Dr. Ellis—they're his, you know."

"Yes." She gestured into a back room.

"Two copies, then, one for each of us."

Ellie said, "And I'll copy the German girl's diary, as I can't have such a rare book leave my library."

Sara agreed. And they set to work at the copy machine. Now Sara knew how many pages there were to translate. She was excited.

CHAPTER TWENTY-ONE:
THE GERMAN GIRL'S DIARY

Returning to number 7, Sara settled in to read the photocopy of the German's Girl's Diary: "My name is Charlotte. I will write in English because I learned to speak and write it at my girls' preparatory school in Vevey, where my parents sent me in 1932. I want to go to America when this war is over. If I save enough money, I will do so. Please, God, let me get through this war alive.

"I work at this club in Rougemont. I talk to the men who come here to watch us dance and to talk to us. They are lonely. Some want sex. I don't do that. At least not yet. I earn money by being a hostess, and talking, but mostly listening to them talk about themselves, their loved ones back home, and about this awful war and their reluctant role in it. Meanwhile, my parents write to me about life in Stuttgart as the war goes on. Sometimes their letters get through the German censors at the border, albeit delayed, sometimes for weeks, before reaching the Swiss post and then I get them."

Sara read on: "My parents say they are happy. Everyone in Germany is happy, so they say. The armies are victorious everywhere. They receive packages of food and other valuable items from my brother, who is with the army in Norway. They go on free vacations to the Baltic in the summertime and stay in a new resort built on the seashore—part of the government benefits offered to Aryan German families. They have been given furniture taken from their Jewish neighbors who were sent to a correction facility." The German girl went on: "I believe these are the things they must write in order for their letters to pass the censors, so I ask myself what is the real story, and I answer that I may never know. Nor will I know what they think of the war and their government. I know the Jews are being sent away. The rest sounds too good to be true. But a free vacation? Of course, my brother is getting one, off there in the German army occupying Norway."

"What about the men who came here to the club?" Sara asked out loud. Appalled at the German population and what she presumed to be their support of the war, Sara read more in Charlotte's diary looking for references to Rougemont. Then she came across this:

"The German Consul in Basel took the train here to ski. I talked to him at the club. He told me that Hitler's is planning his new capital city, called Germania. They are going to build it after the war. He is having his architect Albert Speer design it, and it is going to be glorious. He showed me drawings Speer had given him.

"He stayed with me two nights last week. He said he'd visit me again when he comes to Rougemont next month. He talked about attending meetings at the chateau outside town. I think he just made up the story about skiing. He's a nice man for a Nazi, but he doesn't seem much like an athlete."

This diary is an incredible source, Sara thought. She wondered if anyone else had seen it. Dr. Wolfe said she'd heard about it. Had it been tucked away in the Rougemont Library all these years?

Sara read more about the girl's encounters with the men who had frequented the club during the war. It was a detailed account of each man, their allegiances, their hopes, their fears, their dreams. The German girl commented, "I wonder how many of these men will survive the war, some to go to America, some to return to their homes. Those who don't make it through are destined to lay in a field somewhere, wounded, dying, maybe dead."

Sara pulled herself together and donned her outdoor garb. In the moonlight of a beautiful Swiss Alpine night, she walked around the Chateau a dozen times, asking, probing, wondering what evils had taken place inside its Medieval walls during the war. Evil was pervasive in those days. All over Europe, and even here in Switzerland. Rougemont means red mountain. Yes, blood red for perpetuation of the awful war by the world's central bankers. On the morrow, with luck, she'd learn more from Ellie's translation of the other diary, one written hopefully with more perspective on the events occurring within the chateau itself.

CHAPTER TWENTY-TWO:
THE SECRET PEOPLE OF CHATEAU ROUGEMONT

The following evening in the Rougemont Library, Sara opened her computer and asked Ellie, "Can you tell me who authored the folio pages. Is it a servant's diary?"

Ellie put the folio on the library table and said, "I've looked at a few pages. At first, I thought two or more men wrote it, but now I think it's only one man. His name is Kurt Vogel. The first entry is February 1941." Ellie held up a finger. "The handwriting gets a bit weak as time goes by. The same signature is on every page." Ellie pointed to the signatures. "See here."

Sara saw the German handwriting. "Ellie, Kurt Vogel must be my grandfather!"

"Really? That is most remarkable! Did you ever dream of such a thing? Tell me, how old would your grandfather have been?"

"Old, but, I mean, how old is old?" Sara thought. "Mid-thirties, maybe."

"His German is dated, his references are old, of the period."

"Is that a problem for you?"

"Not really. As librarian, I get all ages of men and women talking to me, so I'm used to their expressions and references." Ellie picked up the first page of the diary and said, "Let's get started." Ellie began to translate the handwritten German, as Sara typed on her keyboard:

"February 1, 1941: "This will be my diary, so long as I am able physically and can find the time to write—even if it is late at night here in my room 7 in the servant's quarters. Here, when I am off duty, I can avoid the watchful eyes of the BIS central bankers who are socializing while I am working in the chateau. My name is Kurt Vogel. I am a member of German Royalty, descended from the Urudi, the ancient 15th century royalty that owned many palaces and much of the land. Together, we ruled the former Germanic states. I was part of the ruling class. My former name is Kurt von Reichard.

"I left Mockmuhl, our home for generations near Stuttgart. I was fearful the Nazis would decide to take me into custody for what I feared was too big a percentage of Jewish ancestry. Many of us, whether Jewish or not, or with even some percentage, have become hyper sensitive regarding our ancestral lineage following passage of the Anti-Semitic Nuremberg Laws in 1935. I knew one of my ancestors was Jewish, and though she was also royalty, we've come to learn that social status makes no difference to the Nazis in their purges.

"I came here to Rougemont because a royal acquaintance of mine, actually a customer of the bank where I worked, had already fled Germany and was living here. I knew about her from a clever pseudo vacation postcard she sent me from Gstaad, pretending she was on holiday, extolling the beautiful skiing on the slopes, and urging me to bring my skis and come see for myself. Appearing innocent enough, her message passed through Gestapo censors. After receiving her card, I decided to look like an authentic Alpine tourist. I bought a pair of skis, packed my bags and, with her implied urging, I escaped the Fatherland."

"Am I going too fast?" Ellie asked.

"No, I can keep up."

Ellie continued translating: "Once here, I found a job as a domestic servant. Me, a member of royalty, employed as a servant! Imagine my emotions! If my royal contemporaries knew, they would look down on me for being unfaithful to my class. But I needed the money and a place to live in safety. Back home, so I have heard, most royalty have been persuaded, or co-opted, to join the Nazi Party. Hitler offered some an officer post in the military, others a diplomatic assignment, or a bureaucratic job, always in return for their royal endorsement of the Nazi Party and, especially, of Hitler himself. Though he has always been suspicious of royalty and secretly wanted to imprison most of us, he tried to take advantage of our family relationships to the British royal family. Some say he was hoping to conduct what would be favorable peace negotiations with England through these royal channels.

"In my opinion, over time, German nobility has taken too much for granted. So much came to us simply by virtue of birth. We were not accustomed to working for a living. I'm adjusting, and I want to chronicle the experience of being here. These BIS bankers are important people. I've come to learn they are financing the war going on around Switzerland. They control gold resources of many nations. What is so important historically is what they are doing with each country's gold. And it is taking place right here. I am able to listen in on their conversations. Much of the time they don't seem to notice us servants unless they want us to bring them something.

"These central bankers are socially prominent people. They are accustomed to having servants tend to their every need. The head of the BIS, Thomas McKittrick, is an American lawyer. He told me he is from a prestigious law firm in New York. He wasn't interested in my background. He asked no questions of me, didn't care where I'd come from, or that I was German. He's too important to care about any of the servants, their stories, or their backgrounds. He told me he is accustomed to having the creases in his morning newspaper ironed out by his butler before the paper is presented to him on a silver platter. I've never used an iron, but I'm learning.

"Six others are employed as servants. Too few for the jobs expected of us. The following are the others who live in the gabled quarters next to the chateau: Hans is a footman from nearby Chateau D/Ox. He worked at the Hotel du Parc when the BIS moved there from Basel and took over the entire hotel, albeit ever so briefly in the summer of 1940 (at great expense, so he told me). He followed the bank personnel to Rougemont from Basel.

"Ursula is a laundress. She brags about her ample supply of soap at a time when everything is rationed. She has several irons and a trouser presser. She is frightfully overworked. The bankers keep unpredictable, odd hours. Their wives are accustomed to having their wardrobes washed and pressed daily, shirts starched, as well as their dresses pressed, especially for their children and, for some, the grandchildren. Ursula showed me their trunks, which were packed with clothes and belongings when they had them shipped on the train from Basel.

"Frau Elena has been here the longest. She was the cook for the American owner of the chateau, William Hallam Tuck. Elena cooks and cooks, collapses of fatigue, and then cooks some more— breakfast, lunch, dinner, the occasional midnight feast. She's in charge of Mr. Tuck's well-stocked wine cellar. Every evening, I bring up the special bottles the bankers request. Often I pitch in and help her serve these meals. Of course, none of the guests has ever cooked, or done any manual labor, so it seems, other than carrying out their duties as important lawyers and now as bankers. We royals have enjoyed similar lifestyles, so I can relate to their looking down on servants as I labor to satisfy their every request.

"Hilda helps Elena with table decorations for dining and with setting the tables with Mr. Tuck's silverware, which she seems to be continually polishing. She lights the many candelabra before dinner. She grows flowers for the bouquet arrangements for each table and gathers fresh wildflowers when they are in bloom. She helps Elena with serving the meals.

"Werner is an hostler. He shuttles BIS personnel, families, and luggage to and from the train station in a horse-drawn carriage. He's lived here his whole life. He's an expert mountain climber and something of a botanist. He knows all the Alpine trails. He leads the bankers and their families on casual walks up into the foothills and forests to look for wildflowers. Based on his instructions, on days when he goes to the station, I sometimes lead a hike, carrying water and refreshments in my pack for the bankers and their families, and especially the little children.

"Eva is a chambermaid. She makes the beds every morning, changes the sheets daily, if she has time. She too is always working. I help her as time allows.

"So, at night, with what energy I have left, I will endeavor to chronicle the life of these central bankers and their families. Some of their countries still cling to neutrality, such as the Swiss and the Swedes. While others, even though their nations and their armies are at war with one another, live here in this safe haven peacefully and seemingly on a friendly basis in this wartime venue of Chateau Rougemont.

"Their purpose in being here—which I have understood is the purpose of the BIS—is to move gold from one central bank to another, as agreed upon in their negotiations. As the attentive servant, I am standing tall off in the background but observing and listening to their discussions. I am often present at their bridge games, and occasionally on their hikes. I listen to every word. I speak enough English plus some French and a little Italian to follow their conversations. No Japanese, but the Tokyo delegate, who traveled here by way of Berlin, Yoneji Yamamoto, speaks English and German. After all, money and banking and gold make up the one international language, as I am becoming acutely aware.

"I might as well be a spy. Not for any country. But for history."

*   *   *

Ellie said, "How are we doing, Sara?"

"Getting your words into my computer as fast as you translate." Ellie popped the top off a Swiss Coca-Cola bottle and poured them each a glass. It reminded Sara of staying up late to cram for final exams. After their sips, Ellie went on:

"March, 1941: I want to note for my diary, in the unlikely event that someone, even many years from now, may read my notes about the bankers who are here, or who come on the train from Basel to join the others, that these BIS men are participants in a select group of lawyer/bankers not involved with any of the military forces fighting each other across Europe.

"For the bankers and wives who need to return to their country, their journey may not be easy. For example, the English, such as Montagu Norman head of the Bank of England, as well as Maurice Frere, the Belgium central banker, whose bank is now in exile in London, and the Dutch central banker, Marquis de Vogue, must leave Switzerland and travel by train across Vichy France to Marseilles and then by ship or plane to England. Or else, they make their way across Vichy into Spain and then to Lisbon, bribing or cajoling for passage on a flight or a ship to London. All the while hoping their plane is not shot down or their ship torpedoed.

"Of course, the German central banker, Emil Puhl, easily crosses the Swiss border north of Zurich and rides first class in a luxury train to Berlin. The Italians have it easy, as well, for they travel through Lugano in southern Switzerland, cross the border at Chiaso and ride in comfort on an express train to Milan or Rome. When Per Jacobbson from Sweden goes back and forth, he travels by train through Berlin and then by a Swedish liner across the Baltic to Sweden, a safe journey, Sweden being neutral. He takes his daughter, Erin, with him. She has told me about their travels and a number of interesting things.

"Not one of these central bankers is an economist. A surprise to me, as coming from a line of bankers, I thought this select group of international bankers, by definition, must understand economics. However, Erin laughed at me when I asked her in our first meeting if her father was an economist. She advised me that even her own father relies only on his gut instincts and his legal training when he makes banking decisions. Neither he nor any of the other bankers has ever sought advice from economists. Nor, she opined, are they guided by any sort of moral standards, other than their own personal consciences as to their legal decisions regarding the BIS. I have come to think their actions fund the central banks of the aggressive powers.

Sara interrupted, "How did the American McKittrick travel here?" Ellie looked up from the folio. "In 1941, he would have come through Vichy."

"But, the Germans occupied Vichy. They would have closed the border with France, blocking escape and entry routes."

"That was a year or so later, I believe. You can ask Lena. She may recall her mother's stories from the war."

After some time, they called it a night. Sara felt warmer with the ski jacket and thicker gloves Ellie had lent her as she walked past the railroad station and the old church, through the chateau's courtyard to her Spartan retreat.

The following morning, Sara read through her transcription of Ellie's translations. At the Tourist Office, she would ask Lena to tell about her mother's World War II experiences.

CHAPTER TWENTY-THREE:
LENA'S MOTHER

Lena told Sara, "The BIS bankers and their money supported my mother's club during the war years. The men came, that is, the ones without families, even some with, so my mother related. Plus Nazi spies and couriers from other countries, who came by train, mostly from the Swiss capital, Bern. There were also some of the supposedly secret American intelligence men, including rescued American and British pilots. She told me that some planes were hit by gunfire from German planes but managed to limp into Switzerland before crash landing. Some planes, regardless of whose air force it was, simply got lost and ran out of fuel."

Sara asked, "Did your mother ever mention an American pilot named Bob Richards, a captain?"

Lena thought. "Captain Bob? Yes."

Surprised by the answer, Sara ventured, "What did she say?"

"Mother told me he came to the club. I believe he was special to her. They would talk about a lot of things… beyond the war. She liked him." Lena smiled. "But then she liked most of the men. Except the Germans, whom she feared. That was her problem."

"How do you mean?"

"Mother befriended many of the men; she saw some as men who might become a partner—not just as objects for making money by connecting them with one of the girls." Lena explained, "In those days, the girls were war refugees. They came here starving, seeking work as dancers… or anything."

Sara asked, "What about my grandfather, the man who became your father?" And then wished she had not asked. Too personal, she chided herself as she saw Lena turn away.

"My father!" Lena exclaimed. She frowned. "I'd like to forget him!"

Sara thought the time had come for her to leave Lena's office. She started to get up, but Lena held up her hand. "No wait. I can tell you one story about the American Thomas McKittrick that Mother told me."

"Please share."

"You asked Ellie how McKittrick traveled to and from Rougemont after the route through Vichy France was closed by the Germans when they occupied what was left of France."

"Vichy was established after the French surrendered in 1940."

"And headed by the revered World War I French general, Marshall Petain."

"So, how did McKittrick do it after Germany took over Vichy and closed the borders?"

"He was allowed by the Nazis to travel through Italy."

Sara said, "But after December 1941 and the Japanese attack on Pearl Harbor, the U.S. went to war with Japan, Germany, and Italy."

Lena grew serious. "You see, Niece, that's the significance of Chateau Rougemont—these central bankers were transferring vast amounts of gold behind the scenes. It made every one of them extremely important to the Axis powers. Even to those powers who were supposedly neutral. Each of the BIS bankers enjoyed special privileges."

Lena went on, "My mother told me that these central bankers from the various countries that made up the BIS all knew each other back before there was any thought of a second world war. They had had many conversations and meetings with each other about banking matters and gold reserves. In those days gold was the basis, the backing, that is, for every world currency. But during World War II, the BIS changed into a band of rogue bankers. They were no longer the typical banker you might know back in your hometown. This band's music was money, the clink of gold bars playing together in a melody sung only by them. They drank the elixir that flowed worldwide from the trough of banking. In the process, they gilded and burnished their professional reputations. In the elite world of banking, they were highly esteemed."

Sara made notes as Lena smiled and said, "The war didn't stop banking or decrease the value of money. Nor did it stop the movement of gold back and forth among their banks, even when their countries were at war with each other. That is what these bankers did right here in Rougemont. They bragged to my mother about their accomplishments, extolling their own personal importance in world banking circles, especially in the wartime arena—the war that was killing millions and destroying nations while—right here where we are now, in the town and in the chateau—they were consorting, one with the other. They were collaborators."

"As they moved gold to finance the war," Sara said.

Lena said, "In my mother's opinion, she became convinced that these central bankers accepted gold from the Nazis without questioning where it came from. They gave them paper currency in return. You can't spend a gold bar. At least I've never had a customer try to spend one here."

"You'd take it, wouldn't you?" Sara said and smiled.

Lena laughed. "Of course, but at what value? Back then values were different. You see, as my mother explained, when the Nazis conquered a country, they seized their central bank's gold reserves. Then the Swiss and the BIS bankers bought it. That kept the Nazis in spendable cash. A lot of the gold they sold to the BIS was stolen from millions of Jews they slaughtered in the camps."

Sara said, "Making Rougemont a bloody red mountain?"

"Yes indeed. Mother told me—she learned these things from the men who came here—that before the war, McKittrick's law firm had many European banking contacts through Chase Bank in New York. It also had a large number of industrial clients in Germany and Italy. The American lawyer arranged financing for a great deal of German industry, beginning right after the end of World War I until even after the U.S. entered World War II."

Sara said, "This story is not in any history books I've read."

Lena said, "I don't know about that. Usually our mother-daughter conversations came after an emotional disappointment she had with some man who frequented her club, a guy for one reason or another she had wanted to befriend. The experience would push emotional buttons, you might say. Due to his eventual abusive actions, she'd come to detest him. Her disappointment would trigger a rant. That is, except for…"

Sara mentally filled in her grandfather's name, but then quickly realized that last bit of news from Lena had concluded the World War II stories for the moment as her aunt abruptly left her office to attend to pub matters. From the direction of the kitchen, Sara heard

Lena's voice, commanding, authoritative, bordering on a disciplinary tone to the food staff. Hers was not the softer tone Sara had come to treasure.

As she listened to Lena instructing the staff, Sara felt that perhaps her aunt was becoming a substitute for the person she wished her mother had been when she was growing up. Taking charge, yet loving. Strong, yet tender. Intellectual, yet practical, traits her mother had not had or was she being too harsh? Alas, Sara wondered, why was she judging her own mother? Did she, as a daughter, have that right? If so, what did she really feel about her mother, a mother now so far away both emotionally and geographically?

Pondering her question, Sara walked briskly back to her number 7, trying with each strong step to sort out both the world war and her own personal matters.

CHAPTER TWENTY-FOUR:
PICKING WILDFLOWERS

The next night, Ellie translated more diary pages. These entries told about how the BIS families took wildflower excursions. In them, Grandfather Vogel reported: "On several occasions, I have led one of the hikes accompanying the bankers, their wives and children on wildflower strolls along the meadow and mountain trails emanating from Rougemont. Today's was memorable:

"Erin Jacobbson, the young daughter of the head of the Central Bank of Sweden, was carrying Martin Nil's Guidebook of Swiss Mountain Wildflowers, to which she often referred. She and the American McKittrick got a little game going between themselves to identify each flower they came upon. Leading the group, I would point ahead to a new discovery with excitement, and usually Erin would exclaim in glee, suggesting its name. But McKittrick, who fashioned himself an expert, would in most cases disagree with her. And they would laugh together and then consult Nil's book again as they pointed out the peculiarities of the new flower in comparison to the book's picture and description.

"The five petal white Alpine Asters were first identified as a species of daisy by Erin, but McKittrick corrected her with what I presume to be the correct name. I marveled at how the five petals were made of a pair of petals, each flowing out from the yellow flower in the center. I had to admit to myself that I'd never stopped in any of my earlier hikes, back when I first came here to study the flowers.

"I recall coming upon a lone and complex purple flower with thorns blossoming upon a stem, which they each readily identified as Rock Jasmine. We lingered around this beauty for some time to allow every hiker to snap photographs with their Kodak or Leica cameras.

"I think the highpoint for me was a wonderful white flower with a yellow center, the name of which they could not agree upon.

McKittrick finally called it an Alpine-milk-vetch. Reluctantly Erin acquiesced, and they laughed, Erin saying something like, 'It's the beauty not the name that captures our attention.'

"What fun these families from many countries had during that beautiful day, even though some are at war with others. What enjoyment I derived by observing their enthusiasm for each of the many varieties of wildflowers, a fascination which was quick to be adopted by the others, regardless of nationality, whether German, Italian, or English. While the day's experience was brief, it proved a welcome break in my tedious routine and hard work of helping the six other servants in managing the chateau for so many self important international guests."

*   *   *

Later that evening, Ellie translated quite a different sort of diary entry, this one from 1943: "Yesterday Werner drove three men from the station. I thought it strange when I heard male voices coming from the servants' door of the chateau. New arrivals who Werner collected from the station were always important people. They would enter through the formal carved wooden double entry.

"I was taking afternoon cocktails to others in the Great Hall when I saw that these newcomers were joined by McKittrick and Puhl. The expanded lot, talking so quietly that I could barely hear what they were saying, made their way up to a private meeting room on the chateau's top level. As I heard them climb the stairs, I eased closer. I recognized two. One was Count Chiano, Mussolini's son-in-law, who is one of Benito's foreign ambassadors. I'd seen his picture in newspapers before I left Germany. The second was Allen Dulles, whose picture I saw in a Swiss newspaper. He is the American intelligence man stationed in Bern. I overheard the third man commenting on the Allied armies relentless fight northward up the boot of Italy.

"A nervous-sounding Chiano interjected that he feared for his life as Mussolini was growing despondent with the Allied armies advancing toward Rome. He feared the dictator was going to blame him, as Benito's paranoia was engulfing those around him. Many in the fascist government were being ostracized, some even losing their lives. The others suggested he flee here to Switzerland. Chiano allowed that, under his precarious personal circumstances, he was giving such a move serious consideration in order to save his life.

"The third in the trio was familiar to me. Once he looked at me displaying a glint of recognition, I recognized from his demeanor—his body language, his insightful look of importance, his surveying the room (and me) as if he were omnipotent and above most of the others, at least by birth—that he was a fellow royal. As he commented to the others about his latest meeting with Hitler and Mussolini, I realized that he was the count from Hesse-Kassel recruited by the Nazis to fill an important diplomatic post. He had become, through personal maneuvering, Hitler's confidential liaison to Mussolini.

"The five men entered the private room and closed the door behind them. Soon I was summoned by McKittrick to bring drinks. I took their orders, one by one, and as I was leaving, I heard Count Chiano mention a German general by the name of Wolff, whom I gathered from his description, was in command of German forces fighting the Allies in northern Italy.

"When I returned with their drinks on a silver tray and some Swiss cheeses, I heard Dulles say to McKittrick, 'General Wolff tells me he is ready to negotiate a separate Nazi surrender of all the German troops in Italy. It will end the Italian part of the war.'

"McKittrick said to Dulles in a somewhat subdued, yet still argumentative tone, 'But, Allen, the American President has declared that the only way to end the war is unconditional surrender on the part of the Axis powers.' He paused and asked, 'Can you disobey the President?'"

"Puhl interceded, saying to McKittrick, 'We must, in carrying out our primary banking duties, think about the post-war period.' Puhl conceded, 'For those of us who follow our military setbacks on the Russian Front, we are beginning to believe that the war can no longer be won by the Reich. My mission as head of the German Central Bank, and indeed our collective mission here at the BIS is to preserve as much as possible of Germany's industrial might and, in the ensuing peace, to restore the bombed portions of our industrial complex.' He looked at McKittrick and said, 'Thomas, certainly you of all people must keep in mind your New York law firm's many industrial clients in Germany.'

"McKittrick nodded, I thought knowingly. He looked at Dulles and said, 'That's why, Allen, perhaps your separate negotiated peace with General Wolff, after all, is becoming so important. Yes, maybe I do personally support it.'

"Puhl said, 'It is important for us to keep the Russians out of Italy, to prevent them from supporting the communists who are trying to overthrow Mussolini. If that happens, Western civilization will cede Italy to the Bolsheviks. That would prove disastrous for all property owners, for royalty in every European nation, for our banks, and our privately owned industry. If it comes to that—Heaven forbid—likely France will be next to go red. Followed by post-war Germany... and...'

"Chiano's facial expression showed his agreement. Nervous about his personal situation, the count abruptly spilled his drink. I went to bring him another. As I headed toward the door, the German royal nodded discreetly at me, and I to him, our exchange connoting royal recognition. While royals have a certain intuitive way with each other, I don't know what he made of me working as a servant.

"As I was leaving, I heard Dulles say, 'A separate peace treaty for Italy is in all our best interests, gentlemen.' I saw their images reflected in the mirrored glass panes of the door as I headed toward it to leave, and the nods I saw came from all.

"When I returned, Puhl was telling everyone he would see that the encouragement for a separate German surrender in Italy was communicated forthwith to General Wolff. Looking at McKittrick, he said, 'In my further thinking about the preservation of German industry in post-war Europe, I am dedicated to working to save as much BIS gold as I can. The bank's wealth must be made available to finance our industry so as to protect it from the Bolshevik threat... after the war, that is.'

"McKittrick nodded in what I took to be his consent.

"I'm no diplomat or statesman, but it was most apparent to me, and I'm sure to each of the men in that room, that Dulles was defying his own Commander in Chief in Washington in working for a separate peace with the German army in northern Italy."

Sara whistled. Ellie laughed. "You're surprised?" To Sara's nod, Ellie said, "You Americans are so naïve."

Sara shot back, "We're principled, idealistic."

"And naïve."

"Do you say that to the men who come to you for translations?"

"Of course not. You only say to them what they want to hear—like what you say to most American men. Right? Right!"

"Not me. It's what you say to me, Ellie. That is what I want to hear."

Ellie smiled. "Yes, Sara, it is what you must hear."

"I'm listening."

"Then hear this." Ellie pointed to the bottom of the page from which she had been translating. "See this asterisk? It was added at a later date."

"Yes, I see. Does that mean my grandfather wrote an amendment... after the war was over?"

Ellie confirmed. "It's dated 1947."

Anxious, Sara said, "Then please read it."

Ellie read, quoting Sara's grandfather: "I must add to my diary so as to include pertinent information I have just read about the Allies and their trials of Nazi war criminals in rubble-strewn Nuremberg. Among those Nazis who were at Rougemont from time to time working for the BIS, as it moved more gold to Berlin, was Emil Puhl. He has been put on trial and convicted of crimes against humanity. He has been sentenced to death, which I'm guessing will later be commuted to a lesser sentence. I write that because I ran into the same German royal liaison to Mussolini I saw in the chateau that day. He was on the train I was taking returning to Stuttgart early this year. We remembered one another from Rougemont. He confided to me the following, which I have written in an amendment to my wartime diary. I sent the amendment to my fellow servant Werner, asking him to insert it into my folio in the chateau because I was giving a lot of thought to going to America. He wrote back and assured me he had. He also wished me a good voyage and congratulated me on my new Swiss baby."

Sara choked up. Quietly she spoke his name out loud, "Lance," and then got back to business by asking, "What does Grandfather tell us after the war is over?"

Ellie read: "The shift of war sentiment among the Allies—the US, Britain and France—has changed from punishing Germany for the war, for their atrocities against the Jews and others to fearing what the Russians will do. Now we are no longer afraid of Germany ruling Europe, but of the Communists taking over Western countries. The West is afraid left-wing political activists in each European country will first win in free elections, having riled up the voters, and then align themselves, both economically and idealistically, with the Bolsheviks. They will immediately confiscate all private property—both corporate and personal—in favor of state ownership to comply with their ideology. Naturally, we Germans, especially we royals, don't want that to happen any more than do wealthy Americans or Brits. 'Just think,' the ambassador said to me, 'speaking as one royal to another, of the investments American companies have made in Europe even from before the war. They still have those investments in place—Ford has a factory in Cologne that turned out vehicles for the German army. It was never bombed even though most of Cologne was laid waste by repeated aerial raids; IBM is in Berlin; Chrysler is in Belgium; and so on. The list is long. Western Capitalists want to preserve those investments and save their property from being confiscated by the Reds."

Sara said, "In other words, financial interests are paramount. It's Capitalism. Greed. Property. Is that what my grandfather is suggesting?"

"That's what the German ambassador he met was saying," said Ellie. "Other people have said it, as well. Sara, you must hear the rest of his amendment." She continued translating. "In addition to the Allies wanting to put Nazis on trial for war crimes, there are people—Americans—who want to also put Thomas McKittrick on trial for collaborating with the Nazis, helping them find a market for their stolen gold during the war. They want to charge him with helping finance the German war machine. They think he should be tried, convicted, and put in prison for being an American traitor. While the Allies officially had imposed an embargo on German gold in 1941, people here in Switzerland, in Chateau Rougemont, including McKittrick, kept doing business with them. In 1942, 1943, 1944. All the way up until May 1945."

Sara sat stunned.

Ellie said, "I need to stop there. I've got to go home and take care of my husband. Don't stay here too late. We're going to have a snowstorm tonight."

"Okay," Sara said, feeling a bit overwhelmed and lost in thought about the men and some women, who made history here with their allegiances to gold, wealth, and property preservation in the Capitalist countries. Such an orientation to gold seemed to Sara to undercut the heralded reasons for fighting the war, which was meant to stop Hitler's insanity. She asked herself, what became of the patriotic causes for which so many men and women died? Her answer was that these causes were plowed asunder like a panzer tank rolling over crops ready for the Fall harvest. But maybe Capitalism is what life in the West is based on—people being able to do what they want with their money, that is, if they're fortunate enough to have some.

Sara stayed behind and continued writing, trying to understand the events that had taken place in Rougemont. Were they as oblique as the happenings from that period of history? Finally, she noted wryly, "his story" was not "her story." How might she view her grandfather's narrative from a woman's perspective? If money makes the man's world go around, what makes a woman's world go around? Love, family, children? She didn't have any of those at the moment. Nature? The environment is beautiful here. Other women? Of course, there was Aunt Lena and others at the pub. And her friends back home.

CHAPTER TWENTY-FIVE:
CAPTAIN BOB RICHARDS

Sara left the Rougemont Library in the wee hours of early morning for her walk back to the chateau. She had assured herself that she had proper winter clothing to confront a storm. Besides, it wasn't a long walk and by now she knew her way even in the dark of the Swiss night. Sara peered out the library window and saw that the sky was clear with an endless array of stars, a sky clearer than the universe of her cluttered mind.

A voice, an older male voice, intruded on her present moment. It was not Dr. Ellis at this late hour come to drive her back. Nor was it a voice she recognized.

"Ms. Vogel," the raspy voice was saying to her.

Sara turned to see an old man in workman's attire, broom in one hand and dustpan in the other, a dark cap somewhat obscuring his face. She recalled that once before late at night she had seen a man in the library, the night clean-up worker, she had surmised at the time. But they had never talked.

She smiled at him. He announced, "My father was Werner, the hostler at the chateau during the war." She remembered the list of servants' names and replied, "Oh, yes, he transported BIS bankers and their families to and from the station. And your name—"

"—Is Papa."

"You were here?" Sara managed, somewhat in disbelief. He must be 90, she thought. "You don't look to be—"

"—But I am—89. And, yes I was here. I overheard some of Ellie's translation of the diary, and it's all coming back to me—those days."

Asking, almost pleading, Sara said, "Tell me more, Papa."

Papa leaned the broom against the library table and emptied the dustpan into a small bag in a debris bin. He tied the bag's loops together and then sat down on Ellie's chair next to Sara. Gently he put his gloved hand on Sara's arm and said, "You're going to write about those days, aren't you?"

Sara nodded.

"I though so."

Sara waited, expecting Papa to say more which he did, leaving his gloved hand on her arm, as if he were afraid she'd leave without him saying what was on his mind. "Ms. Vogel, what took place here during that awful war—as I remember my father impressing upon me—was what the world was all about in those days, and maybe still is today, and that is gold, wealth, money, and the power that gold brings to men. Gold and power." Papa repeated himself, tears forming. "Ms. Vogel, you must tell the world." As if he had intruded, Papa removed his hand from her arm and pulled a great coat over his body, found his cane, and turned to walk out of the Rougemont Library and into the Swiss night.

"Thank you," Sara said. She gathered her material and donned her winter jacket. On his way out, Papa raised his arm and saluted her.

* * *

Leaving the library behind her in the dark of night with it's glistening crystals of snow, Sara thought again about her grandfather's account of his overheard conversation between Thomas McKittrick, and the English central banker, Montague Norman. She recalled their words:

"I realize, Montague, that in 1938 after Chamberlain's Munich accord with Hitler, in which he ceded the Czech Sudetenland to Germany, all of us were in the mood of continuing to appease the Nazis. That feeling, which you and I shared with so many other bankers in the BIS and politicians from most countries, except perhaps Churchill, was that, benefiting from Hitler's signature on the Munich document, we, along with all of Europe, could look forward to, as Chamberlain having gotten off and standing by his airplane, smiling proudly and waving the agreement, proclaimed, 'Peace in our time!' The resounding cheers from the throng gathered to welcome him home to English soil reverberated around the world, soothing tensions everywhere."

"Norman replied, 'Indeed, that was the pervasive attitude, well… really the hope of the day. That sentiment of appeasement and cooperation with Germany guided our ensuing actions, at least for a short time, but not for long. After Chamberlain's declaration, we at the Bank of England continued to follow the BIS charter and its rules guiding what we were legally charged to do.'

"McKittrick said, 'You're thinking about the transfer of the Czech national gold?'

"Norman nodded. 'Yes, we—each of us—at that time believed we were legally bound to follow the BIS rules that had been adopted by our central banks and ratified by our democratically elected parliaments.'

"McKittrick said, 'As a lawyer I agree that we are morally bound to obey the rules of the BIS charter. I always say if it were not for the rule of law, where would civilized society be?'

"Norman reassured, 'So true. You know, Thomas, thinking back about it and the criticism we suffered, in hindsight we at the BIS were legally required to deliver the Czechoslovakian gold to the Nazis. We removed the Czech bullion from the special vault in London where, fearing war and for safety's sake, it had been stowed earlier by the Central Bank in Prague. So, off went that nation's gold to the Reichsbank in Berlin.'"

At this point, Sara recalled, Ellie had translated her grandfather's personal commentary about the incident: "The trouble I'm having with McKittrick's adherence to the rule of law is that he ignored the morality of the situation. He, Norman, and the BIS allowed Hitler to capture the Czech Central Bank's national gold, even after it had been removed from Prague and securely stored in the London vault of Norman's Bank of England, from where Norman gave it up. That gold gave Hitler his much-needed financial boost to start World War II barely a year later with the invasion of Poland. After the Czech gold was appropriated, Hitler's regime had the money to pay in gold for its much-needed weapons, ammunition, plus copper from Sweden, coal from Switzerland, and all the other commodities Germany didn't have. The Nazi dictator could tap the international commodity markets, whether in Portugal, Spain, Argentina, or wherever. The raw material shortages in Germany were no longer an impediment to his war effort. He could go anywhere to fill out his shopping list for vital war goods. Had Hitler not had that gold, maybe he would never have had the financial strength to start the war, let alone continue it."

Mulling over her grandfather's words, Sara continued her by-now-familiar walking route… until looming up ahead she saw the Medieval church that Ellis' granddaughter Melissa had described upon arrival in Rougemont. The church was closed, of course, but in the peaceful night Sara couldn't help but wonder about the sermons once delivered there. What had been the many prayers offered to a higher authority, to the god of the Swiss? All those years ago, what had been the hopes and fears offered up, hopefully seeking relief from suffering? There was so much suffering in those days, she reasoned. Yet she wondered if, 75 years ago, during the awful Second World War, life here was any more advanced that it was in the Medieval ages? Though she listened intently, no answer came from the silence surrounding her in the middle of the Swiss night.

Passing the pair of weathered wooden entry doors, Sara felt a gust of wind slap her face.

Suddenly she was transported back to another time and to the scene now confronting her. She felt snowflakes on her face. The flurries increased as she passed under the arch, which brought her into the chateau's courtyard. Falling snow had obscured Ellis' car. Barely able to see through the swarming flakes, Sara squinted at what she sensed was the chateau. She knew it had to be there. Ahead of her. Yes, there it was, in its ghostly architectural grandeur. From its side, Chaucer's Chanticleer rooster peered down at her through a brief void in the flakes, seeming to almost crow to her.

Snowflakes fell on Sara's nose. To her horror, she saw that the flakes were red, not white—each one! More flakes came—all red. Making her way closer to the chateau through the falling snow, Sara observed flickering light emanating from the many windows. The light served to illuminate her path, while bestowing a reddish-yellowish tint to the snow falling all around her. Amidst the flurries, a dark figure passed in front, not seeing her, hurrying, carrying something.

Sara eased her way through the floating flakes to the closest lighted chateau window. Brushing away the red flakes from the pane, Sara pressed her face as close to the cold glass as she dared. For warmth, she tugged her ski jacket up around her neck.

Peering through the window, she could see from the many flickering candles and the electric chandeliers that the chateau was furnished with the familiar antiques she had seen in one of Ellis's folios. Women and men were walking about, some standing, talking to one another, cocktail or wine glasses in hand. The women wore designer gowns, the men tuxedos or dinner jackets. Sartorial elegance abounded. Young girls romped in sweet calf-length dresses. Others sat in little chairs reading books. Young boys, fashionably attired, played on the carpeted floors with toy trains. Some in lederhosen had tucked toy guns into their belts. Two older boys wore shirts adorned with Nazi crosses. Sara guessed these two might be carrying real guns. Aghast, she watched as they brandished their weapons and shouted, "Heil Hitler" with right arms raised and palms outstretched. Feeling compassion for the boys, Sara stood for a moment watching them.

From inside, the candles seemed to speak to her in a firelight of welcoming warmth. She felt a sense of continuum, as if she belonged both here in the now and here in the yesteryear.

Sara moved on to the next window and saw antique game tables, likely English or French, all with polish glistening. Sitting around the tables, foursomes were playing cards. Bridge? Must be, deduced Sara, recalling Ellie's translation of a passage from the diary about the belligerents playing bridge during their stay in the chateau.

Suddenly, Sara sensed another presence near her. Was it a person breathing? Or was it the wind blowing? Sara froze. Dare she turn to the right, or look to her left, or behind her? Might it be Dr. Ellis coming for her, concerned about her being out in the storm? Might it be…? Was it anything? Anybody at all? Or just her fears? Her anxiety about the place? Or the strangeness of this almost out-of-mind experience? She couldn't be certain she was having a real experience. She doubted the moment. She almost doubted her very existence.

Sara listened and thought she heard someone speaking. Not from inside the chateau, not a voice from the warm interior on the other side of the cold window glass. Instead, from her side, outside, a low voice. Not subdued. Rather, it was authoritarian—knowing, wise, and deeply male. The voice was telling her something. From the tone, it must be an urgent and a significant message. Whose voice could it be? Who was the stranger with the message?

The voice whispered, "The cards. Look at the cards." Sara squinted again to see through the windowpane, trying to identify the cards being held by the people playing bridge. A deck was about to be shuffled by one of the men. Yet the deck was thicker than the one they used in the Student Union at JWR.

Sara watched the cards being dealt face down to the four players. A woman's back was to the window, allowing Sara to see the cards as, one by one, she picked them up and slowly began to arrange them, suit by suit. Surprised, Sara saw she was sorting five suits, not four. Sara saw clubs, diamonds, hearts, spades and… What was the fifth suit?

"A Swastika!" the voice whispered to her.

Sara stiffened. Not from the cold. Not from the red snowflakes covering her parka-clad arms and shoulders. The voice, strong yet intimate, said, "The fifth suit. Do you see?" He waited for Sara's nod and her hesitant question, "But why five—"

"—It's all the rage in this year of 1942. My mother in Indianapolis wrote me about it. Everyone's playing bridge with five suits, not four, everywhere, worldwide."

Slowly, Sara looked away from the window, turning her head toward where she thought the voice was coming from. Yes! He was there. Taller than she. Handsome in his military uniform and attractive with his presence. His magnetism drew her like gravity. Her knees weakened. She tried to smile. He didn't. She tried to speak. She couldn't. He did. "In America, the fifth suit is Eagles. In England, it is the Crown."

Recovering, she whispered, "And in Germany… is it the Swastika?"

Captain Bob Richards smiled, for now she realized that's who he was. He said, "It is five suits the bankers and their wives are playing with in there." Cryptically he added, "In Chateau Rougemont, the BIS has added a fifth dimension to this war—gold. They've made up their own bankers' rules. Goes beyond tanks, airplanes, submarines, and guns. It's the game of gold. It's their fifth suit."

She said softly, "In Switzerland, the neutral central Bankers—"

"—Are not neutral." Then he was gone. No longer by her side. Sara felt his absence. An overwhelming loneliness overcame her. Even though she had been on her own in her Swiss assignment, she had not felt so alone as at that ice-cold moment. All along Sara had felt a certain comfort in the sensation, knowing that Lena, Ellie, even her father, were somehow with her. As was Professor Kinkaid and Erika Wolfe. And yes, her grandfather, through his diary, even if it was written 75 years ago. He was with her, at least in spirit. Dr. Ellis, too, and maybe even the other girls at the pub. All along—until now—she had been with people. Captain Bob had come to her side, spoken to her, and just as mysteriously vanished into the snowy night. The resultant feeling for Sara was that she was being left standing, alone in the snow and peering through windows. She was looking back into a time period where she couldn't possibly be. By his leaving, she had been left by herself in this distant past, and in this wintry present. Alone in a snowstorm of red snowflakes. Alone in all of time.

Sara's emotions plunged into a rapid downward spin, buffeted by what she realized was a kind of virtual reality world. She recalled a speaker at college, visiting from the big state university, who had given a lecture about VR. Of course, that day he had brought along the necessary headsets and glasses. In an exercise as part of his talk, she and her fellow students tried them on as the lecture proceeded. And, presto, they had travelled into another dimension, viewed another world. But here peering into Chateau Rougemont at this moment, she had no headset, no special glasses. Just her ski hat and herself. And, she sighed, handsome Captain Bob. She told herself she was experiencing the virtual reality of traveling back in history.

Sara moved through the snow to the next window. Inside, to her surprise, to her instant joy, she saw him again, Captain Bob Richards in his dress Army Air Force uniform. How could he, one man, be so attractive? Yes, he was looking at her through the same window, seeing her face, she realized, and she seeing him. He was inside the chateau with the BIS bankers, their families, and the servants whom she saw continually bustle about, bringing drinks, snacks, or just being there, waiting on call for orders to fetch something for somebody.

Looking toward him, she saw that her hero aviator was continuing to look in her direction. His strong smile traveled through the window to consume her attention. Yes, he was specifically looking at her! He held up his arm, his hand extended toward the window. His index finger made the motion of summoning her inside, enticing her. Should she enter the chateau? Yes! Be with him again! Of course, she would! She did, through the rear entrance she had used earlier during her first visit to the empty Chateau Rougemont.

Once inside, with the candlelight flickering and reflecting alluringly in his eyes, he came nearer to her. Immediately, it was as if Captain Bob instinctively knew the exact, the right, the proper, the most exciting of all moments to put his arm around her. Sara felt his male strength, sensed his mystery, welcomed his warmth on this cold night. Even through her ski jacket.

He said gently yet firmly to her, "Walk among the tables. You will recognize the players from the photographs you saw earlier in Ellis' quarters. Listen to their talk. Mostly English, European English, not Hoosier-speak. Within a few minutes you will understand the motivation that is behind this war. You will experience the deaths, sense the concentration camps. You will feel and breathe gold. All of these things I have come to know by my being here—so far from home, our home, oh, to have this war over and done with and to be back home again in Indiana… and the Moon Upon the Wabash…" He kissed her. Gently. Then more firmly. Then full firmly. And she him. And Sara desired all of him. Yearned for him. Craved him as never before she had craved any man. A fresh new feeling. A cascade of emotions captured her, as the two of them, in her senses, to her pleasure, clung to each other, two foreigners in a strange land, linked by heritage, by emotions, by history.

But then, as suddenly as he had come to her side in the storm, as quickly as he had embraced her inside the chateau, he was no longer in her presence. Gone.

Once more gone. She felt a sinking feeling in her soul. Sara was alone. True, other people were talking, drinking, playing bridge, drawing her attention. There were also the seven servants, one of whom must be her grandfather. Which one was he? Here among the guests, perhaps the hurrying form she had seen passing in front of her carrying something as she approached the chateau? Yet to them she was unnoticed, an unseen young woman, obviously not one of them. Not noticed and not feared by any of them, she walked among the bridge players, observing, listening, mentally recording their conversations, registering the scene and the traits of each person to be later transcribed into her notes that would later form part of her eventual dissertation.

The chateau's décor was rich with antiques furniture and notable works of art. Sara walked gracefully through the opulence and the opulent people, the central bankers of the world and their families. Eagerly, hopefully, she moved on, searching each of the many chateau rooms looking for Captain Bob attired in his dress American aviator uniform. Alas, having searched the rooms without success, she gave up, reluctantly confirming, in truth, she was on her own in this important time so many years ago.

As it had been with her wartime aviator hero, whom she knew was with her barely a few moments ago, each of the central bankers was indeed present. She stood behind them, watching one by one as they bid their hands, played their cards, drank their liquor, talked their talk.

"I bid six spades." "I bid six Swastikas." "I double." "Re-double." "Note the double and re-double on the scorecard," someone commanded. The cards, all five suits, were promptly laid down by the dummy.

CHAPTER TWENTY-SIX:
THE PLAYERS

T*he two strutting boys, showing off their lederhosen, marched smartly past the table beside where Sara stood. Oblivious to her presence, with their right arms raised, fists clenched, they shouted out in unison,* "Heil Hitler!"

"My wonderful grandchildren," Emil Puhl, director of the German Central Bank, proclaimed loudly. Playing his hand's opening card, he told the others at his table, "As you can see from these two young men, our Hitler youth are more fit, more athletic, and more disciplined than children in your countries." His stern looking wife dutifully nodded. Watching her banker husband tuck away the first trick of the hand, she smiled, albeit briefly at his astute playing, and then returned to her stern countenance.

Thomas McKittrick grimaced at Puhl's successful finesse and said rather apologetically, "Our boys are going through rigorous basic training."

McKittrick's wife, the hand's dummy, dutifully smiled in agreement.

Moving from table to table, Sara began to notice each woman's jewelry—rings, bracelets, necklaces… all expensive. She reflected on their personal wealth. Their opulence. She felt, no sensed, then saw the high degree of self importance conveyed by each man. Yes, and each woman… through her jewelry… her attitude… her poise… her demeanor. Suddenly Sara felt insignificant, humbled, to be in their presence… well, to feel their presence. She began to philosophize. Here in Chateau Rougemont, it was the men who were dealing secretly amongst themselves in gold while the women sorted the suits in their hands. That was what was visible, but behind the scenes, or just subtly, the women were doing a lot more in their marriages by bolstering the men, through their presence and support. But not through criticism. Nor guidance. Nor even hints of leadership. Sara asked herself if each female, regardless of the worth of her jewelry, had been dealt and was dutifully playing the hand of the dummy in their respective marital partnership.

Returning briefly to her contemporary time frame, Sara asked herself, How could she properly address the role of men and women in history? How could she properly portray women's role amidst all this personal gold? How could she tell their story in this man's world of glittering wealth? Had the women goaded the men to lavish them with jewelry? Or had the men entrapped the women with promises of jewels? Were the women just there for sex and the production of babies? Lena's mother had apparently feared becoming some Aryan baby machine if she remained in Nazi Germany. Instead, she had fled. In this night back in distant time, Sara admired the women's wedding rings. Yet, how much of their gold jewelry —at least for the German and Italian women—was stolen from the Jews and others deported to the death camps?

Sara thought about the camps and remembered an alarming story Erika Wolfe had told her about the most infamous German concentration camp. In 1941, a German citizen who lived near Auschwitz had witnessed thousands of persons being delivered by rail to the camp and had seen smoke rising from the crematorium. Deeply concerned, he had traveled to Zurich to personally inform a leader in the Swiss Jewish community. In turn, the Jewish leader had circulated the grim story throughout Switzerland and had attempted to convey the news to the Allies. He was shunted aside by Nazi sympathizers who still abounded in Switzerland and, yes, even during the war years in other neutral countries, as well as even in those at war with the Axis powers. The result among the American diplomats in Bern, Erika had said, was to discredit the story and ignore it.

Having heard the story from Dr. Wolfe, Sara had winced. How could the Holocaust have taken place? Her father's expressed nostalgia for the 1930s suddenly seemed blatantly misguided. But the story about the Jews being persecuted was far more than just some wild rumor, given the details that Erika had cited. Yet at the time, nothing had come of the German citizen's eyewitness account of the death camp in Poland.

What would she, Sara, have done about the story if she had been alive back then? Would she, too, have kept quiet? No, of course not. But was she a hero, in those days perhaps a heroine? And what would her father have done had he been alive then? Was each generation a function—a product—of its peculiar times, trapped therein? Isn't that why we study history, Sara thought, in order to escape such a trap? But surely, then as today, individuals can decide to act, to do things that make a difference.

Sara reflected that the white snow falling on Chateau Rougemont in the 1930's might have been purer than today—maybe there was less pollution in the air. In springtime back then, were the wildflowers more colorfully brilliant? Noise levels from traffic were lower perhaps. People were less harsh in their comments. Or maybe none of those differences were evident if a comparison were possible. Maybe as Dickens wrote, it was indeed the worst of times, and maybe, today was the best of times.

Sara felt, on behalf of a sudden and certain loyalty to her generation, a gnawing responsibility to improve the world. She was here on an important assignment. Yes, she might be able to do her part if she could continue her research about the events of World War II and write something encompassing and informational and new about the events that took place here in Chateau Rougemont. Sara continued to observe, yearning to understand what her mission was and what she was to write about.

Thinking back as to what she had read about the Holocaust, Sara contemplated the huge quantities of gold the Nazis had pried from Jews' teeth, stolen from the possessions of homosexuals, gypsies, and political prisoners—the liberals, Socialists and Communists—the non-conformists to the Nazi myth who had been sent to the gas chamber. Finding herself reluctantly resigned to the truth, Sara surmised that in reality these millions of unfortunate people had given up their gold, their possessions, their property in order to finance a Nazi war intent on establishing Aryan domination over Europe and even beyond.

Sara watched as the proud Puhl took another trick. He laughed and boasted, "I've already made the double doubled. Lots of points go to me!"

Sara moved to another table. Here the fifth suit was "Crowns". English, she surmised. Remembering the old photographs on Ellis' wall, Sara recognized the head of the Belgian National Bank, Maurice Frere. He was speaking to Montagu Norman, head of the Bank of England. "I'm so pleased that we have been able to maintain the stability of gold throughout the war, regardless of who controls what territory. I mean, my country's national gold is safe." He paused and reflected. "At least I think it is. Anyway, I know it's not in Berlin... at least not yet... I hope and pray."

Norman's wife said, "But Monty, didn't you tell me on one of our wildflower hikes that the Belgian gold is now in the hands of the Vichy government somewhere down there in French Africa?" She grew serious as she turned her attention away from bridge. "Why is it, Maurice, that all this gold, the wealth you men deal with daily, is more important than the lives of the brave men and women fighting in the front lines and being killed in dive-bombing air raids on cities, dying on battlefields from machine guns and exploding mortar shells?"

Maurice shuffled the thick deck and began to deal another hand of cards. "How can you say that? Of course, it's not. But still, Hermoine, the precious metal gold will continue to be the world's currency when all this fighting stops, no matter how long it takes for one side or the other to prevail on the battlefields. Regardless of who wins, gold will reign as the ultimate monarch over all of Europe. Under BIS guidance, gold will be ready and waiting to finance each of our post-war economies."

Hermoine said, "You mean after this awful war is over, if it ever is, there will be some sort of re-building effort to restore the homes and shops ordinary people have lost in so much shelling and bombing?"

"Yes," he told her, "even the Germans are looking to protect their interests after the war ends. Of course, if we listen to Herr Puhl over there, the Germans think it will be their world. However, given the German retreat in Russia, some of their leaders—maybe even Puhl—are beginning to realize the futility of the war they started."

Hermoine asked, "Why do you say this is their war, a German war?"

Slowly Maurice sorted his cards by suit and by high-to-low denominations before looking intently at his wife and then at Monty and saying, "It's obvious, isn't it? It's their war because it's their reaction to losing the First World War— The Great War, the war to end all wars. That's what the American President Woodrow Wilson declared after America got embroiled in the conflict in 1917. This war is the German revenge for what they believe were the unfair terms of the Versailles Treaty of 1919. That treaty, of course, is why we are here tonight playing bridge in this beautiful chateau—the reason the BIS exists, as I am sure you all realize."

Before bidding, Monty's wife asked, "They started the war to get their gold back? Is that what you are saying?"

"Yes, in a way," Maurice said. "They wanted to rebuild their country despite the billions of dollars of reparations to the Western Powers they were forced to pay under the terms of the Treaty." He emphasized his comment by forcefully slamming his next card down onto the table, "Yes, they were obliged to pay the reparations entirely in gold!" His voice rose as he reiterated the word, "Gold!" He added, "Not with paper bonds, or printed paper currency, or promises for the future, but in the ultimate hard currency, gold bullion. Pallet after pallet of ingots, each shipped by the BIS, were delivered to the victors' central banks. Under the

Versailles Treaty, in the 1920s and 1930s, the Reichsbank delivered reparation payments in gold ingots to Britain, Belgium, and France. "Then," he said, "those countries repaid their respective war debts to the United States in gold."

Monty said, "Germany has always been short on commodities and the weaponry needed to carry out the war effort. They must buy these goods from other countries in various parts of the world and pay with real money. That means gold. So, yes, they wanted their gold back in order to restore the health of their economy, provide for the welfare of their people, and assert themselves militarily."

Maurice said, "To rearm, build their air force, buy tanks and trucks from Ford and technology from IBM and weapons from Bofors in Sweden. In order to conduct this war, they needed gold. Gold is the law of the BIS and the law of economics everywhere. Gold is how the Nazis are financing their war. They are seizing gold from the central banks of countries they overrun. They supplement that with gold from the sale of art from the unfortunates they are killing in the camps." He looked at the cards in the hand he had dealt himself and said, "You know, gold ought to be the name of the fifth suit that trumps all others in our bridge games in this chateau. The king's crown is gold." He went on, "The pursuit of gold is the reason for this war. The Germans need gold and they need a war to obtain it, either legally, or else steal it. Their credit, you see, is shot. They are essentially bankrupt, and have been since Hitler came to power. From the effects of war reparations, the unlimited printing of money, internal strife, inflation, riots, unemployment, lawlessness, the national treasury has been further depleted. Other people's gold is saving them. We central bankers here at the BIS are facilitating their efforts."

"Monty said, "Don't say those words to Herr Emil Puhl." He gestured two tables away where the two Hitler youth were showing off their goose stepping. Montague shook his head, smiled at his bridge players, shrugged off the youths' antics, and said, "You know, I'm content we central bankers here don't have to answer to anyone other than to ourselves about our actions in moving mountains of gold—not to newspaper reporters, not to politicians, to no one at all."

Maurice nodded his assent. "I rue the day that will ever happen. Just think of some reporter—"

"—Who doesn't understand banking—"

"—Exactly, Maurice. If they do report anything having to do with money, gold or economics, they get it wrong. Show me a reporter who understands any of these subjects, certainly not banking. You can't. Anyway, that'll never happen. No reporter will ever ask us questions. Our private club here has the entire banking world to ourselves."

"But, dear," Hermione said to her husband as she visually examined and

sorted her five-suit hand. "Tell me again, what has become of our Belgian national gold that the Nazis hoped to confiscate when they invaded our country? I thought it was safe when, as you told me, in anticipation of war, we shipped it into the custody of the French."

Maurice, first to bid as the next hand was dealt, offered an attention-getting two no-trump. Then he said, "You are right, that's to whom we sent it, believing it would be safe in their vaults. The Vichy French government, who received our gold, moved it down into one of those Free French territories in Africa. Enraged, the Germans have demanded it be delivered to them. And since the Vichy government is under the thumb of the Nazis, they are in the process of ordering the crates loaded onto camels. Their plan is for the camels to caravan the gold across Africa north to Casablanca where they hope to ship it by boat to Marseille and then by train to Berlin."

"Why don't we stop them?"

"Because it is all legal. Your country's gold is in Vichy French controlled Africa, and we're not at war with Vichy."

Sadness evident in his voice, Maurice said, "I argued with McKittrick. Yet he assured me the BIS is doing the legally correct thing by allowing the Germans to seize our gold from Vichy. In their documented formal request—per BIS rules— the Germans followed the proper legal procedures spelled out in the our charter, which was agreed to by all the major powers back in 1930 when the BIS was set up."

Hermoine shook her head in sadness. Then she asked, "What about those poor souls hiding out in the forests of Europe to avoid being captured by the Nazis?" The table's contestants grew silent, looking at her in disbelief. But she went on, "My former maid, Adrianne, a Jew, sent me a letter from Terezin, that camp in Czechoslovakia. She wrote about her life. They were visited by the International Red Cross, but the Nazis staged a massive cover-up, fooling the inspectors into thinking the Jews were being well taken care of. She also said her teenage son, who had escaped from Brussels when the Nazis invaded our country, sent her a letter, telling how he and hundreds of other refugees were secretly hiding out, roaming the forests of Moravia in what used to be Czechoslovakia before it was divided by Hitler into the Protectorate of Bohemia and Moravia."

No one commented on her observations or questions. Instead, the game went on, silent trick after silent trick, the rules of the game prevailing.

Sara wanted to ask each of them, especially the women, to disclose their deep feelings about why gold was so important to them personally. She wanted to ask how much gold jewelry, or maybe silver, they each possessed. She wanted each of them to tell her why such value is placed on gold and its intrinsic value, when so many people in Europe and Asia and Africa had died for it, and many more were surely going to do so this very night while the four of them played their card game. As they were shuffling the deck, bidding, trumping and taking tricks, people were being killed, shot, gassed, dying of starvation, hiding out in forests for fear of being caught either by the Nazis or their sympathizers to very likely be sent to the gas chambers.

Overwhelmed by each bridge table conversation that she was struggling to understand and all the while taking mental notes, Sara sensed mounting repulsion to the scene in the chateau. She was seeing it all take place before her very eyes and ears. Levels of anxiety about her assignment rose and mixed with a rage at what she was seeing. She thought about Jack. She thought about all the victims of this war, even though it ended 75 years ago. She felt compassion for them. And then she felt dizzy. War victims crowded her thoughts.

Disagreeing with the bankers' statements extolling their roles in banking caused Sara to pose questions about the origins and causes of the war; questions of morality of the nations and their leaders; questions as to why the war was swirling all around the borders of Switzerland, so near geographically yet so far removed; questions as to why so many soldiers and civilians had died; questions as to the widespread suffering of millions who, through no fault of their own, got in the way of gold and its many inhumane paths; questions as to the reason so many representatives of warring belligerents were cordially playing bridge together in this Medieval chateau in Switzerland. Sara was beset with confusion and uncertainty.

She stood there, invisible to them, while they were vividly alive to her. Uncertain, she looked for Captain Richards. Nowhere. She was on her own, but not in spirit. He was here somewhere, as was her grandfather, who was poised ready to serve these bankers, no matter what mundane request they made for drinks or food.

Sara moved to the next table. Right away she recognized the French central banker and his Italian counterpart. From their over-the-top makeup and provocative attire, Sara concluded the women with them were not their wives, but instead dancers from Lena's mother's club—girls who knew how to play bridge and other games, as well. The fifth suit of cards they were playing with, she observed, was the Fleur-de-Lys. Cigarette smoke rose from the players at the table as they puffed up a storm. From time to time, the girls lit the men's cigarettes, laughing, smiling at their consorts, and being the ever-so-titillating hostesses. She wondered if today gold continued to represent the ultimate goal of wealthy men. What about women? Was it their goal, too?

*   *   *

153

Seeking relief from all these questions, Sara turned away from the scene of the interior of the chateau to gaze out the windows. It was a relief to look toward this new vista, the great wide world. She admired the night's idyllic winter landscape. The snowstorm was over, and the scene was illuminated by a brilliant moon. She was standing outside again. No red flakes were falling. Pure all-white snow covered the ground. The welcome fresh snow embraced fields stretching forth beyond the chateau and up into the magical Alps. She had found her way back to everyday reality. Sara welcomed the relief to escape from the bankers, their five card suits, and their focus on gold.

Nevertheless, she was going to have to write about them. It was her assignment. Her job now. Her career. Her chance to contribute to history, to add to the formal record being kept by Clio in the great archival house of the muses. The Library of Congress. Or in college libraries. And the halls of academia.

Sara turned back to look again through one of the windows of Chateau Rougemont. To her surprise, a different scene greeted her. The bridge players were gone, along with their decks of cards. The beautiful art and vintage furnishings had vanished. All that was left was the cold, darkness, and silence of mid-winter. Sara felt miniscule. She was suddenly adrift in the passage of time separating her from the events of the 1940s.

Her realistic and intuitive experience had taken place so many decades ago. The card games the bankers had played had been dealt, scored, and put away. The glitter of gold offered in those days had been either fulfilled or forgotten. But then, looking higher on the exterior wall of the chateau, Sara saw the rooster Chanticleer. It was now glittering with golden wings, its feathers' gilt casting a mien replacing the candlelight from the windows she had seen only moments before. Yes, she concluded, Chaucer's rooster was reminding her of the important role gold had played within its chateau during the war.

She recalled that each player in the games had appeared to be consumed with the search for tricks, for gold, while adhering to the governing laws of banking, rather than the humane laws of society. Lives had been ruled and ruined by their worship of the precious mineral. Was gold the root of evil and the cause of the world wars as well? That was Professor Kinkaid's thesis, his argument, his life, and the reason—well, maybe not the entire reason Sara was here.

Bracing herself against the cold winter night, Sara began to expand on the many ideas she would write about. However, she wanted to follow her usual method—for assurance and her own self confidence—which was to have one final chat with her professor, to reassure herself she was on the right track. Before beginning to write her dissertation, she reminded herself that not only was it protocol, but that she wanted to confer with Professor Kinkaid and Erika Wolfe and share her thoughts and ideas, seeking their guidance.

It was much too late to call them now. The hour and the night's onslaught of amazing experiences were consuming her energy and mellowing her thoughts. Yearning for sleep, Sara turned and made her way toward her room number 7, leaving behind a trail of footprints in the fresh white snow.

CHAPTER TWENTY-SEVEN:
CALL FROM ERIKA

Sara's cell phone rang, disturbing her deep early morning slumber. It was too early in the morning to talk to anyone. The ring wouldn't stop playing "Back Home Again in Indiana" unless she answered. On the screen she could see that it was not a call from Indiana, but rather a Geneva city code. Dr. Wolfe's name appeared. She decided she'd better answer and managed to mumble a groggy "Hello."

"Good morning, Sara, this is Dr. Wolfe. Skip and I want to check in with you. How you are getting along?"

"Ah, I'm sorry if I sound sleepy. I was up late last night—doing research."

"Good, Sara. Progress, or not? Diary? People? Insights?"

Sara said slowly, "Yes... all of the above. I found the legendary diary. Dr. Ellis had saved it from the movers, Elsa, we all her Ellie, is translating it for me. And the German Girl's diary was found by Ellie in her library. It's in English."

"Two diaries! That's marvelous!" Erika said. "Sara, I know this is short notice, but can you summarize your findings in a brief email to me by this evening? We're having an Institute board meeting tomorrow, and I want to report on your progress."

"I've been up most of the night... working on the translation of the diary."

Wait, Sara warned herself, how much dare she reveal of her experience? She wanted to add, "And with my World War II pilot, with whom I've fallen in love, I've been watching the BIS central bankers and their wives play bridge with five card suits at the antique game tables in the chateau." But she didn't say any of that. If she had, she knew she'd be asked to explain, and she was too tired to make a logical attempt to put her unorthodox personal experiences into some sort of reasonable, and hopefully understandable, perspective.

Instead, she paused, her uncertainty prompting Erika to ask, "Sara, are you all right?"

"Oh, yes, Dr. Wolfe, quite okay... splendid. I have lots of information to work with, lots of ideas kicking around in my head. You won't believe some of the connections I've stumbled upon." She wanted to disclose how an American pilot whose plane crashed during the war in the field next to the Chateau, his co-pilot dying in the crash, had shaped her research. Of course she didn't go on to say, "He survived and avoided what would have been wartime interment by the Swiss because Allan Dulles intervened." Instead, she told Erika, "Yes, I found the diary—it's quite long and in German with lots of details about what took place during the war among the bankers and their wives and children living in the chateau."

Sara heard Dr. Wolfe call, "Skip, I'll put us on the speaker." Professor Kinkaid's voice came on, "Sara, how are you? Where do things stand in your research?"

"Oh, Professor Kinkaid. I'm fine. A lot to tell you about." She felt a bit more awake. "I'll compose an email and send it when I get back to town and Lena's Pub later today. No Internet here."

"A pub? Sara, where are you staying?"

"I'm staying in the servant's quarters at the chateau? The pub is in Rougemont. It's Lena's Pub." She did add, "I've learned that Lena is my aunt."

Sara heard Erika's worried voice, "How can that be? Skip, our poor girl's in some sort of difficulty." To Sara, she asked, "Shall I send a car for you? Maybe a doctor?"

"—No, no, I'm okay. I've been taking notes from Ellie's translation of the diary before she goes home to care for her husband. But as to the bridge games the bankers and their wives were playing, they were with five card suits..." Sara paused. "Geez, Dr. Wolfe, Professor Kinkaid, I'm sorry. I'm not making much sense, am I?"

Silence from Geneva. Sara thought she heard a cork pop and then the sound of flowing liquid. "Neuchatel," she suggested to herself. "This early in the morning!" She chuckled to herself, adding to Professor Kinkaid, "Sir, I'll summarize in my email... when I walk back to Lena's Pub and can get on the Internet."

Erika came on the phone to say, "Once I get your email, I'll report your progress to the Board. Good work so far. At least it seems so, don't you think, Skip? Sara, we better have a reunion, and with your father, too. I'll make the arrangements."

Sara said, "Give me another week to wind up the diary's translation. Then… yes… a reunion… in Basel. Yes, at the BIS with my father. I want to confer with all of you before I get too far in the writing." Sara said good-bye, clicking off her cell. She promptly drifted off to a welcome and, for her, a continued and well-deserved sleep.

CHAPTER TWENTY-EIGHT:
SARA'S REUNION

They gathered high atop the Bank for International Settlements in Basel. Her father's driver had picked her up as she stood in the taxi line at the train station. Once inside the BIS, Erika met her at the elevator, hugged her and escorted her up to the top of the tower to a cozy lounge. Framed photographs of men from years past, including a few women from the present, looked down upon them as they entered. In judgment? Admiration? Combatively?

Professor Kinkaid and her father Lance were already there. Three older adults and one younger woman. Ages apart. Entering, Sara noted but gave the diverse chronological ages little note, thinking only of her important historic assignment—the dissertation she was determined to write. She hoped it would result in a path toward a literary calling.

Seeing her father, she voiced tenderly, "Lance." Father and daughter embraced. Sara took him aside and whispered, "I must tell you what I found out from Lena." Succinctly she related the family story that Lena and she had discovered.

Reacting, tears slowly beading in his eyes, Lance said, "My father... I never knew his real story. Your grandfather. Unbelievable." Reflecting further, he said, "Fills in a blank page in my life's story."

Sara noted his tears. To her surprise, she saw a new and emotional side of her father. She said, "Mother will want to know." He nodded. She said, "I'll tell her when I fly back home."

To her surprise, Lance hugged his daughter. "Sara, I've never been much on family. Never knew my father's background or who my mother was. That is, until now." He dabbed his eyes with his monogrammed linen handkerchief. He looked closely and tenderly at Sara and said, "You've given me a new fondness for family... your efforts here. I'm so proud of you."

Erika Wolfe poured wine and announced, "Courtesy of BIS."

Professor Kinkaid addressed Sara, "Could you summarize for us what you've learned now that you've had this opportunity to delve into the events at the chateau. Tell us how your findings have shaped your thinking about war."

Sara sipped the wine and tried to compose a reply as a slew of doubts rushed at her. Maybe she was too young, too inexperienced to make pronouncements on such a major topic. After all, she had only recently graduated from JWR and was just now researching her dissertation. Such conclusions might or might not come to her in the future after further study in her PhD program. Yet she was beginning to cultivate and nourish such thoughts and formulate her own ideas.

Yes, she was enrolled in the PhD program at the big state university in Bloomington. Yes, she hoped to soon have that elevated degree, that stamp of academic status signifying she could teach, write, and publish. But only if she had something worth conveying to scholars, students, and history buffs.

Sara recalled that over the course of her experiences in the chateau and in Rougemont, she had begun to form opinions and explore new concepts. Now Professor Kinkaid was asking her to voice them. Her father, Professor Kinkaid, and Dr. Wolfe were looking at her, anticipating her remarks.

She realized that she dare not disclose her experience traveling back in time. Likely it would make them discount what she had to say. She had to skip that aspect of her experiences. A dissertation couldn't cite such abstractions. Academia was awash in facts, not visions. Opinions had to be based on hard research. Her time travel experiences would have to remain unspoken and unwritten. But, for sure, they would remain in her thoughts and help to focus her mind.

Sara began, "As I told you, I did find the World War II diary. Two diaries actually. One in English by a German girl working in a club in Rougemont during the war. The longer one was written by Lance's father, my grandfather. Ellie has translated it from the German. From it, I have concluded that gold and the quest for it drove the fascist forces to commit atrocities against humanity. The fascists eroded the foundations of civilization that had developed from the beginning of time. Anti-Semitism made it all the worse. Male rulers, politically and economically, were in charge of the world, many, if not all, pursuing their own selfish monetary agendas.

Turning to her father, Sara continued, "Lance, you told me that in the 1930s everyone knew their position in society, but I have come to believe that their roles were miscast. The wrong people came to power. Hitler. Mussolini. As well, the central bankers, who were really lawyers playing the role of central bankers by running the world's gold supplies at the BIS."

She paused, adding, "In today's world, the male drive for wealth, power, and prestige needs to be redefined and redirected—for the benefit of civilization."

She waited a moment. "As for women, in my view, women need to be more assertive in their lives, especially in their relationships with men, including their economic relations with men. That way, women can have more influence on society and more of a chance to make a positive contribution to modern life. If there's one thing the world doesn't need, it's a band of men, all by themselves, controlling the world's wealth with no checks or balances on them whatsoever.

We must learn from the past and aspire to a better future. From what I've learned about the BIS central bankers, they were educated, intelligent, and sophisticated, but they somehow couldn't see the difference between what was legal and what was right. If they'd had a few women economists working with them, maybe they wouldn't have made the same disastrous decisions, but maybe they would have seen that their most important priority was ending the war, not maintaining the gold standard." She smiled at the others.

Her listeners applauded. Professor Kincaid said, "I'm glad you talked to Dr. Ellis. He saved the day for us by preserving your grandfather's diary."

Sara said, "He's a little dotty, but a good man."

Kinkaid said, "Yes, I have come to think he's all right. I have come to believe that all people... well, not all... but most... mean well."

The foursome shared the Neuchatel and Sara said, "The events I will write about did take place inside Chateau Rougemont."

Erika Wolfe said, "Yes, Sara, now you must go home and write your book in your own way, as truthfully as you can. Skip and I will always be available if you want to share your thoughts as you go along."

Sara thanked her four supporters, one by one, and then left with her father for dinner. Now, all of sudden, they had so much to talk about. Her grandfather, his father. Lance's childhood upheaval, leaving his mother and sister behind in Switzerland and moving to America. Sara disclosed that even the BIS and international banking fascinated her now. Lance seemed to her to enjoy having someone to talk to about his work, someone with interest in it.

Before they parted, she invited her father to visit her in Rougemont before she returned to the States. That way she and he and his younger sister, Lena, could have a family reunion. She thought it would mean a lot to each of them. And they could resume their family roles—brother, sister, father, daughter, niece, aunt.

*   *   *

Sara wrapped up her research and flew back to Indiana. After a few days with her mother, she was more open-minded as to her mother's obsession with clairvoyance.

She packed up her belongings and made the move to the campus in Bloomington, where she signed up for two new courses— introductory Economics and German. She began working with diligence toward earning her PhD in History. She already had a good grasp of the subject of her dissertation, which gave her a leg up on most of the other doctoral candidates. The two diaries she found in Rougemont were primary source material other scholars had never studied. For Sara, the diaries were a literary gold mine.

CHAPTER TWENTY-NINE:
SOMETIME LATER
THE BOOK REVIEW
BY FRITZ SHMIDTZ

Sara's book, based on her PhD dissertation, was published by the Institute to End War and widely promoted in the media. A review appeared in two prominent Swiss newspapers, one in Zurich in German, the other in Geneva in French. An email from Ellie attached the review translated into English. The story's headline read, "American PhD Candidate Pans for Nuggets in World War II."

The review read: "Professor Sara Vogel has written a fine historical work, *Mountains of Gold, Storms of Blood*, about the world's most powerful central bankers who lost their moral compass during World War II. She tells the story of how during the war bankers at The Bank for International Settlements (BIS) in Switzerland continued to do business with the Nazis. The BIS unilaterally chose to facilitate the transfer of billions of dollars in gold bullion used to finance the Nazi war effort. Dr. Vogel's historical tale is based on her grandfather's eyewitness account working as a servant for these masters of high finance.

"Dr. Vogel's ability to recreate life in a Medieval Swiss chateau during the war is impressive. The villains, such as the head of the German Reichsbank, Emil Puhl, and the head of the BIS, American lawyer Thomas McKittrick, are imaginatively and convincingly depicted.

What makes this true story especially shocking is the collegiality of the wartime adversaries and their families. They lived and worked together in a remote Swiss chateau high up in the Alps. As the rest of the world waged war, Dr. Vogel's bankers strolled Alpine trails in the afternoons, ate and drank their fill in the evenings, and amused themselves playing bridge with five-card suits. Their willingness to fraternize with one another and to rise above the fray of World War II reminded this reviewer more than a little of Jean Renoir's classic, "The Grand Illusion," except that Renoir's film is fiction, and this story, unfortunately, is firmly grounded in fact. Several historians, after reading review copies, told me that in academic circles Dr. Vogel's work has piqued renewed interest in what the BIS did and did not do during the war. They are calling her research groundbreaking.

"Several historians, after reading review copies, told me that in academic channels the story is being looked into with renewed interest, given the depth of Ms. Vogel's research."

CHAPTER THIRTY:
SARA'S BOOK LAUNCH

"Dr. Sara Vogel" in red letters screamed the banner, "Here tonight" The next line read, "Dr. Vogel will tell a revealing story of WWII in her debut novel!" The bookstore window displayed an inviting arrangement of her books. Sara's glamorous photograph was meant to catch the eye of prospective readers passing by the store window, inviting them inside where they would surely be energized by the vast world of books, as well as by Sara's talk. "Tonight, 7 p.m." in blue letters shouted the pasted-over time alert.

Chairs were invitingly arranged. A microphone atop a podium had been positioned to accommodate Sara's height so she could read certain passages from her work. On a table at the rear of the store, wine glasses were waiting to be filled and cheese and crackers were laid out.

By the time of Sara's presentation, only a few patrons had entered the store, poured wine and loaded up on cheese and crackers.

One picked up Sara's book, admired the cover, saw the chateau and looked at Sara. She smiled in recognition. Some patrons sat. And waited.

The bookstore owner waited. Sara waited. Another customer. Eight now.

Then, after being introduced, Sara told about why she had written her novel, and related the events leading up to her trip to Switzerland. She talked about Chateau Rougemont and what an impressive Medieval building it is. Then she read from two chapters.

One patron said, "Ms. Vogel, please tell us if you have found new insights about why we always seem to be fighting wars."

Another said, "Best book of the season, I say!"

The ninth and tenth customers came into the store, each picking up a copy of the book and flipping through the pages as if they were speed-readers.

And that was that.

Sara hid a tear but went on with her rehearsed talk.

Afterward, she counted ten books sold, each dedicated to the buyer and signed by her. Some customers bought more than one book. For a friend. For a relative "who has always studied the war."

As the store closed, a man in a greatcoat lingered. His hat was pulled down, obscuring most of his face. He approached Sara, his steps hesitant as if he were in some discomfort, perhaps, she thought, even physical pain. He reached out and shook her hand with tenderness, as he discerned that she was disappointed in the evening's turnout and book sales. In a fatherly voice, he said, "Sara, you did your best. You wrote a great book. I have found that, to my chagrin, many folks feel better when they cling to misconceptions. Perhaps they don't really want to know the truth. Truth scares a lot of people." His hand continued to grasp hers as he said, "Be assured you have set the record straight. The important thing is the reason the war was fought, and you have most capably described the forces at work, the craving for gold that dominated the world at the time of World War II." He released her hand before he said, "Be proud of what you have written!"

He turned to leave. She tugged at his sleeve to hold him back She raised his hat and looked carefully at his face. She said affectionately, "Thank you, Mr... uh... uh..." He smiled. She hesitated. "I thought you might be someone else."

"I'm Cecil..." Then, in slow hesitant strides, he left the store lovingly clutching two signed first editions.

CHAPTER THIRTY-ONE:
SARA SORTS IT OUT

After the man called Cecil left, amid the store's display of colorful book covers, the owner busy tiding up, Sara acknowledged to herself that she craved a glass of Neuchatel. Yes, for relief from the nervousness she felt presenting her work in public. And for the days, weeks, and months that went into writing her book. She had spent many hours drafting the manuscript, during which she had reviewed her notes and files, while calling on vibrant memories of her time in the Alps. She had relived, remembered, and, she hoped, drawn intelligent conclusions about the events she had witnessed in Chateau Rougemont.

Now, relieved of the stress of her book talk preparations, Sara yearned for a respite following the many tedious days of page proofing her book, and discussing promotion with her publisher, the Institute. While the IEW was paying the costs of publicity, both internationally and locally, Sara expected assistance in whatever ways she could with the publication process.

As the days passed and she became enmeshed in the myriad details of publishing and promotion, Sara fondly recalled her days in Rougemont, sipping wine with her Aunt Lena and talking about their families, especially mothers and fathers. Then there had been those nights with Ellie working to translate grandfather's diary. Such wonderful memories. Sara missed the excitement of her days in Rougemont.

With a stack of unsold books under her arm, Sara ventured out of the bookstore, in search of a lounge where she could order a glass of Swiss wine, sit, sip, and reflect on her adventure, on her life, and maybe even fantasize about her future as a writer, a researcher, a professor, an historian, any one of which pursuits at this juncture in her life might well be hers.

In the heart of downtown Indianapolis, Sara walked and walked, looking, searching, her books growing heavier with each step. If only… Sara soon felt herself slipping back in time.

An old-fashioned sign read "Claypool Lounge," and it was on the ground floor of a hotel rising above. She thought how, during the 1930s in Basel, the BIS had been sequestered above a chocolate shop. Similar situation, Sara told herself.

Candlelight glow from within the lounge. Entering through the clear glass door, Sara found herself in an old-fashioned parlor filled with vintage furniture— tables, chairs, plush padded sofas, plus planters with ferns. The lighting was subdued, enhanced by the firelight of candles. She found an available lounge chair and dropped into it. Setting her books on the floor, she got the waiter's attention, she ordered glass of Swiss wine.

Sara began to relax, taking notice of the patrons near her. Their clothing seemed unusual, their demeanor, too, almost strange. Had things in Indian changed so much since she'd been a young girl growing up there?

Allowing her attention to shift, Sara began to chart her future. She could continue with the Institute to End War—they had an assignment in Africa for her, but she really didn't want to go to Africa. Not after Switzerland. It just didn't seem right.

Sara's mind drifted as she looked around the room. An old man sat at a nearby table. He was a scholarly looking gentleman. Given her experiences with Lena and Ellie and especially Kinkaid and Dr. Wolfe, Sara was more likely to approach older people. Yes, she'd ask him for advice. And so she did. In response to her query about the future of the world, the man replied, his voice slurred, Girly, izz zat your book?" He pointed. "Is it poetry?"

The attentive waiter interrupted, "Here's your refill, Mr. Riley."

The older man nodded and sipped, then gulped, some of the gin clinging like thoughts of discarded poetry lines to his rumpled beard. Eyes glossy, he looked at Sara and pontificated, "Poetry izz king."

Sara didn't know how to reply. Mr. Riley went on, "That's all I ever wrote—poetry." He smiled. "And they named a college after me. Think they'll ever do that for you?"

*   *   *

"There you are! We found you at last!" Kyra's voice floated across the lounge, a familiar and welcome voice.

Startled, Sara shook herself back to the present. Looking up, she recognized her former JWR college roommate's smile and waved. The two approached each other and embraced.

Kyra quickly explained, "Joe and I wanted to be there for you, but our babysitter was late, quite late actually. That's why we missed your talk and signing. How did it go? Did you sell lots of books? I'm... we're anxious to know."

Kyra was with her husband Joe. Sara recalled having seen the photos Kyra showed around campus. Accompanying them was an older man. Sara recognized him right away from the bookstore. It was the man she had talked to at the end of the event—Cecil.

Kyra said, "We just met up with Cecil here on Monument Circle, as planned—our plan B for the evening." She laughed. "Somehow, he knew we'd find you." Kyra looked at the older man with curiosity and asked, "Why... how did you know where to look for Sara?"

"Nothing like a little clairvoyance, Kyra," Cecil replied, smiling. "Sara and I are tuned to the same channel, or so I believe. You see, the old Claypool Hotel—it's long gone—was once the hotel in Indianapolis. James Whitcomb Riley, in his later years, used to come in here everyday and drink... and drink. Sara may not have actually known about that, but then, I believe that somehow she did and she automatically found this location, which is the site of the old hotel." He paused and looked around. In the Hoosier night, the group was standing and now talking on the sidewalk next to a vacant lot.

Sara remembered, "I tugged at your hat... ah... Mr. Cecil at the signing. I thought you were someone I knew, but you weren't."

"I am who I am, as are you, Sara."

Kyra said, "Cecil's a movie producer... Hollywood, you know. He's here to watch the 500 Mile Race. Doing a movie on it, aren't you, Cecil?"

Cecil said, "Researching, not yet filming. We're going to be watching from Joe's family's private box. It's right there at the narrow row of original bricks that mark the start and the finish line."

Kyra said, "Cecil wants to—"

He interrupted to say, "You see, Ms. Vogel, I lost my dear grandson in Afghanistan. He was... I can't tell you..." He turned away. Then forcefully he said, "I want to get an anti-war message out there on movie screens everywhere. So, I'd like to make you an offer for the rights to your book."

Sara stood silently and stared at Cecil.

"Ms. Vogel, Sara, I want to option your book with the idea of making it into a movie. And I want your assistance working with my screenwriters on the script. I plan to film on-site in Switzerland."

Sara managed to say, "You do?"

To his smile and nod, Kyra said, "Whoopee!"

Sara threw her arms around Cecil's shoulders and hugged him. That was all she could do or say.

Kyra broke the silence. "Sara, Joe and I would like to arrange a second book signing at the most popular independent bookstore in the City. The media will come. Joe's family will see to that! And we'll get all our family and friends to come, as well."

"I'm overwhelmed, " Sara said. 'This is all too much."

Kyra added, "Sara, do you remember that gold ingot in Kinkaid's office—inside the Plexiglas case?"

"For sure. What became of it?"

"Weirdly enough, Kinkaid left it behind and Manny and I salvaged it. We got a good look at it under a magnifying glass."

"And?"

"It's got a Chinese symbol on it. We think Kinkaid got it when he was in the army in Korea and found out how the Chinese financed the Korean War."

"With gold?" Sara asked, receiving in return everyone's nods.

Meanwhile, the old poet weaved along the sidewalk coming toward Sara. She saw him wink and heard him say, "A movie is almost as good as having them name a college after you."

CHAPTER THIRTY-TWO:
SARA BACK AT HER FAMILY HOME

"I'm home from my book signing, Mother."

Her mother ignored her news, saying, "I think I've made contact with my grandfather, my mother's father. Madam Claire and I had an intimate session this evening."

"But, Mother, your grandfather is dead."

"He's enough alive to talk to me."

"Okay, sure. Good night, Mother," Wanting to go to her old room, Sara remembered her high school fantasies about boys and girls, about books, about colleges, about history, how she'd decorated her room. Putting those memories out of her mind, she said, "I'll sleep on the couch in the living room."

"I put out blankets and a pillow for you."

"Thank you, Mother."

Her mother turned to leave. Stretching out her arms, Sara offered a hug only to get in return a departing hint of smile, and she was left alone. Trying to dismiss the rebuff, Sara sat at a little table and opened her laptop computer, intent on checking her email.

Right away, Sara saw a message from Lena, which she promptly read: "Dear Sara, Ellie and I and all the people here in Rougemont send their greetings. Especially me. Your book got a good review in the papers here. Ellie shared it with everyone. Most of us have read the book and take pride in telling people that we are proud to know you, and that we admire your research and your writing.

"But most of all, I'm writing to you with a very personal message. None of my staff knows. My dear niece Sara, I am growing older, much older every day. Take my advice, Sara, and never grow old. Ha! I don't have as much energy as I used to. Now and then, my mind skips a beat. Time is like a raging Alpine stream in the spring sweeping everything away. In short, Sara, I don't know how much longer I'll be able to run the pub.

"As you know, I have no kin here, no one to rely on, other than maybe Ellie, but she's not family and she and I don't always agree on our politics. There's no one to help me, either in my aging, or my pub—that is, in making the decisions so necessary to run either. Your father is away in Basel. I have no one here to help me.

"Sara, I'm inviting you to return to Rougemont, to fly back here. If you will do so, I'll put the pub in your name, even change the name to whatever you want, teach you how to run it, how to oversee the staff. I'll teach you how to collect rent from the tourist office, how to work with the town council and stay in their good graces.

"Oh, Sara, please come back to us, and to me!"

Sara wept openly, but silently. Then she gazed out her bedroom window at the house next door—the house of Captain Bob Richards, where he lived those many years ago with his mother. Sara looked at the house longingly. Memories of Captain Bob, the urge to be with him, consumed her for long and tender moments.

Then across her mind floated the pub's new name: "Sara's Central Bankers' Pub." If she flew back, Aunt Lena would help her make it real.

THE END

END NOTES

The events depicted in this book did take place in Chateau Rougemont. The names of the world's Central Bankers and their families are real. However, since no known personal diaries exist chronicling the events, additional characters in the story, while historically likely, are by necessity fictionalized—except for Captain Bob Richards, my next-door neighbor in Indianapolis. Before America entered World War II, Capt. Richards joined the U.S. Army Air Force, and soon was ferrying bombers to Hawaii. He later died when his plane crashed on Rendova Island off New Guinea in 1942, a year before American and Fiji forces retook the island.

James Whitcomb Riley, of course, was world famous for his poems, including those about Little Orphan Annie, during the heyday of the Hoosier literary period. In later life, as my father recounted to me, Riley visited the Claypool Hotel Bar regularly and drank excessively.

The Bank for International Settlements continues to thrive in Basel and functions with on-going worldwide financial and economic influence.

THE GAME OF BRIDGE

The game of bridge was played worldwide with five suits, not four, in the late 1930s and early 1940s. Names for the fifth suit varied by nation. The U.S. chose Eagles; England had Crowns; France picked the fleur de lys; and Germany, of course, preferred the swastika. That fifth suit, beyond the typical four weapons of guns, tanks, airplanes, and naval vessels, was the "gold" of the rogue central bankers—it trumped everything.

1930S GERMAN GENEALOGY

The genealogical document that bore the swastika, to which Professor Kincaid refers, was a requirement of 1930s Nazi Germany. In Stuttgart in the 1960s, my cousin showed me such a document featuring my family's lineage.

OTHER WORKS BY JON FOYT

Previous Fiction by Jon Foyt (writing with Lois Foyt)

Last Train from Mendrisio
A tycoon sets up an offshore trust

Postage Due
Mother Dear becomes Queen of Albania

Marathon, My Marathon
Nuclear Waste disturbs a cross-border marathon

The Portrait of Time
Native American spirituality competes with an evangelist

The Architecture of Time
Preservation versus a bullet train's right-of-way

Out of Print

The Landscape of Time
The 1808 untold story of the Erie Canal's origin

The Test of Time
A Cleveland socialite joins the WACs in WWII

ABOUT THE AUTHOR

photo by Helen Munch, Victoria, BC, 2013

A native of Indiana, Jon Foyt began writing novels and screenplays with his late wife, Lois Foyt, in 1992. A distance runner, he has finished 60 marathons. He holds degrees from Stanford in Journalism and Geography plus an MBA. He also has completed class work for an Historic Preservation masters at the University of Georgia.

Foyt's other careers have included radio broadcasting, banking, and real estate development in Oregon and California. At 85, Jon is an active participant in the retirement community of Rossmoor in Walnut Creek, California. He has three children, eight grandchildren, and two great-grandsons.

AUTHOR'S CREDO

Jon Foyt does little to promote his work because: A) He doesn't like to self-promote, and B) it takes time away from conceiving, researching, and writing the next novel and the next novel after that.

Instead of allocating time to social network, race after bookstore signings, and plead with book reviewers, Jon, at age 85, says he wants to write about characters who explore topics and situations he feels have been overlooked.

He does hope people will read his novels. Comments can be emailed to him at jonfoyt@mac.com. He will gladly reply. Jon's website: www.jonfoyt.com

BIBLIOGRAPHY
The Gilded Chateau

The following sources were consulted for this novel:

Schloss, Henry H., *The Bank for International Settlements*, North Holland Publishing, Amsterdam, 1956

Bardo, Michael D., Series Editor, *Central Bank Cooperation at the Bank for International Settlements, 1930-1973*, Cambridge University, 2005

Smith, Arthur J., Jr., *Hitler's Gold*, Berg, Oxford, UK, 1989

Talbot, David, *The Devil's Chessboard*, Harper Collins, New York, 2015

Toniolo, Gianni, *Central Bank Cooperation at the Bank for International Settlements, 1930-1973*, Cambridge University Press, New Hork, 2005

Jacobsson, Erin E., *A Life for Sound Money, Per Jacobsson, His Biography*, Erin E. Clarendon Press, Oxford, 1979

Birmingham, David, Switzerland, *A Village History*, Ohio University Press, Athens, Ohio, 2004

Ozgercin, Kevin, *The History of the BIS, 1930-1958*, Dissertation: City University of New York, 2005,

Pays-d'Enhaut, 2014, *Editions Cabedita, Biere*, in French printed in Italy

Lebor, Adam, *The Tower of Basel*, Public Affairs, New York, 2013

Petropoulos, Jonathan, *Royals and the Reich*, Oxford University Press, 2006

Rauchway, Eric, *The Money Makers, How Roosevelt and Keynes Ended the Depression, Defeated Fascism, and Secured a Prosperous Peace*, Basic Books, New York, 2015

Kwarteng, Kwasi, *War and Gold, a 500-Year History of Empires, Adventures, and Debt*, Public Affairs, New York, 2014

Lewis, Nathan K., *Gold: the Monetary Polaris*, Canyon Maple Publishing, New Berlin, NY, 2013, Introduction by Steve Forbes

Urbach Karina, *Go Betweens for Hitler*, Oxford University Press, 2015

YouTube video, *UKTV History, Banking with Hitler*, 2006

BIS, *Thirteenth Annual Repot*, April 1942-March 31, 1943, Basle, autumn, 1943, dated June 18, 1943

BIS *1942 Annual Report*

BIS *1944 Annual Report*

BIS *1945 Annual Report*

Thomas McKittrick papers on microfilm, Baker Library, Harvard Business School

William Hallam Tuck, Personal Papers, Hoover Library, Stanford University

Canton of Vaud, Property Records for Rougemont, author's email correspondence